The
ANATOMY
LESSON

The
ANATOMY
LESSON

John David Morley

St. Martin's Press
New York

Library of Congress Cataloging-in-Publication Data

Morley, John David
The anatomy lesson / John David Morley.
p.   cm.
ISBN 0-312-13426-6
1. Americans—Travel—Netherlands—Amsterdam—Fiction.
2. Narcotic habits—Netherlands—Amsterdam—Fiction.
3. Teenage boys—United States—Fiction.   4. Brothers—United States—Fiction.   5. Grief—Fiction.   I. Title.
PR6063.O7446A82   1995
823'.914—dc20   95-22171   CIP

First published in Great Britain by Abacus

First U.S. Edition: September 1995
10 9 8 7 6 5 4 3 2 1

For Ben, Sam and Joe

The
ANATOMY
LESSON

ONE

I've been frozen solid against the wall in Mazzo's, staring at my index finger for a couple of hours, when my dead brother Morton shows up. He does that literally. I mean, I look down on one side and see him coming up through the floor. Nothing special about that. People have been showing up through the floor all evening. They pop up and mushroom in bursts, clumps of people that explode and disappear. In the Mazzo theme park it's another of those acid nights.

Hi Morton, I go, not particularly surprised.

Hi Kiddo, goes Morton. How about a beer?

Uh huh.

I reason that this conversation is probably not taking place. The music in Mazzo's is so loud there's no way I can hear what Morton is saying in any case, even if he *is* there.

All flesh is grass, goes Morton.

Not these days it's not. *Was* grass, Mort. We've moved on.

Fine, fine. What're you hanging round Mazzo's for?

Like I said: for the LSD and the XTC.

Let's go, Kiddo. You're wasting your life in this hole.

I'll join you at the bar. Order me a beer.

1

Actually, it's like this. I'm stalling because I'm not able to move. I've hypnotised myself with my own index finger. I'm the location on the wall through which everything in Mazzo's has to pass. Light and sound waves bend through me and all the dancers, chequered lights, dance across my body. I don't move a muscle. Senses scalped, heart beating outside my chest, I am the woofer and the dance floor, I am the emptiness that absorbs everything. Spaces are opening up around me and I see Morton — already fifty yards away — heading for the door.

Hey wait!

I'll leave a message on your machine.

Tell me the message now.

See you around, Kiddo.

Morton, wait . . .

But when I come out onto Rozengracht at five in the morning there's no sign of Morton. There's a bunch of people sitting in the road outside the disco and they say they're going aboard the barge in the tunnel down by Amsterdam Central, only the barge doesn't move, so they smoke and stuff, and that's the trip. Great, I say, and No when someone asks if I'll come along for the ride, because I've done that trip and it was boring as hell. Right now I just want to concentrate on myself, and other people tend to get in the way when you want to do that.

Fantastic things are happening over the water. In the canal I see blurred shimmering lines, of houseboats, cables, the quivering masonry of landbound houses — and looking up I see a city convulsed, streets of quivering houses, chimneys trembling and gables wonky, capsized roofs, I see Amsterdam rocking on its marshy ooze.

Terrific, I go, nodding kind of I know – I know – I – know – don't – tell – *me* to myself, but then I get woozy and climb off from that hump-backed bridge which I can feel backing up more and getting pretty damn high. I just walk along the canal and watch the dark peeling away layers till morning's there and suddenly it's light.

It's a summer morning with *a very high voltage* up there in the sky. This is – jeeks! – some kind of street-cleaning operation, I mean, *high*giene. Morning comes in a nuclear flash, scouring the gutters and hitting the pavements with a smack you can see rebounding in zillions of refractions. I hear a clock striking the hour as I bolt out of the passage under the Rijksmuseum, and on the other side I see the trees peeled of their shadows in an instant bloom of light.

The kids are already out there under the trees, the roller-skaters and the skateboard freaks. But there's no action. I stand and watch them through the railings. The kids don't make a move. Two cross-sections of tube stand side by side between the trees and the kids just sit on the platform and don't make a move.

I go: Action!

And they do. I mean, this may just be a coincidence. The black guy who is the roller-skater pushes off from the edge and drops down into the tube. It's not a big deal. He just goes down and up and back down and up and hops out onto the platform again.

The skateboard guys watch this from their stretch of tube without an awful lot of interest. They scratch a while and consider the options. Then one of them hops onto his board and does a couple of ups and downs and hops off, and everyone stays put again.

Watching this through the railings, I'm reminded of monkeys in their enclosures of dead forest in a zoo, the same listlessness, the same mechanical motions in between.

I realise I'm coming down to earth again. I head for the park. Anywhere but home, where giant spiders will

TWO

Most weekdays when the weather's fine I get out to Vondeln Park. At home I do exercises to tone my muscles, have a shower and shave, a spot of something nice and whiffy. Toast, coffee, sometimes a cigarette. It could be ten in the morning, or it could be three in the afternoon. I avoid routine. Routine is the killer.

Sometimes I take my skateboard along and join the kids in the playground behind the Rijksmuseum. When I'm inside the picture, practising flips on the tube, I'm attuned to fine differences in the noise of the wheels, and it all seems to be really neat action. But when I'm outside the picture, just passing by and looking through the railings, all I hear is the monotony of the wheels, don't see much action at all, and I feel the same boredom I guess most humans feel when they watch the primates swinging listlessly round their dead forest in the monkey house.

It's all go at the park. All the welfare brats are lying out there sunning themselves. Some of the guys bring along clubs and do a workout, but I never really got into juggling. In the park I lie and read comics or watch video on the portable Billy brings along. He brings along a portable and a steel suitcase. It's the kind of suitcase salesmen carry around with samples to show their customers. Billy's suitcase contains about a dozen different kinds of grass, all neatly laid out in separate racks. He hangs out every night in Siberia, his suitcase on the counter, selling grass until four or five in the morning. Billy's the authorised in-house dealer. The owner of the coffee shop takes a cut, something like twenty or thirty percent, on what he sells.

Billy's this not quite real American. He's a pretty old guy, thirty-five, maybe already forty. He was in some kind of special marine task force in Vietnam. He killed people with his bare hands. I mean, it was as many as fifteen or twenty. He told me about this at Popeye's one night when we shared a tab. He has nightmares. It troubles him a lot, having to carry those hands around with him all the time. But he's a regular guy.

Billy has this weird idea we should go into business together. He and some other guy have rented a greenhouse outside Amsterdam where they grow weed. Growing and selling weed is the business he wants me to get into. I can come in as a partner. The entrance fee is six thousand guilders. I tell Billy he's crazy. Even if I had six thousand guilders, why would I trade it for my peace of mind? Billy's a country boy from some place like Ohio and at heart he's still deep into the work ethic.

Lying out in Vondeln Park, he takes a stash of high-grade Indian tea out of his samples suitcase, blends and rolls us bazookas. We lie in the sun and smoke, the guys do their thing with the clubs, the girls tan their tits, Billy and I talk.

'Get yourself registered,' I go, 'and take the welfare.'

'I don't qualify for welfare,' goes Billy, 'I'm not a Dutch citizen.'

'Everyone qualifies for welfare. In Holland it's a law. The streets are paved with welfare. You just have to fill in the forms. Respect the bureaucracy, go along with the hypocrisy, and take the money.'

6

'Don't you ever get bored?'

'Sure. It's an occupational hazard.'

Billy thinks that's incredibly funny. He doubles up laughing, and kicks his feet in the air. The high-grade Indian tea is getting to him.

Recently the summers have been getting warmer. You can lie out in Vondeln Park without a shirt on until late in the evening. Sometimes we lie out there all night and I don't get home until noon the following day.

I live in a condemned building in a street off Prinsengracht. A nice area, central, cheap. I pay a hundred guilders for the apartment. That's a tenth of the welfare cheque that comes to me from the state every month, courtesy of the tax payer. It's a good racket, and I've been into it now for quite a number of years.

Not that you start off on a thousand a month. You have to work your way up. When I started I was on six hundred and fifty. The next big increase doesn't come along until I'm in my fifties and due for my pension. That's thirty years ahead. It's worth sticking with the system, although it does require a lot of patience.

The Dutch are big on tolerance. They're big on liberalism. One half of Amsterdam is on the dole and doesn't mind, the other half pays and says it doesn't mind either. Still recovering from Calvinism, they're prepared to let tolerance and liberalism cost them a lot. It's a purge, an enema. They're terrified of catching the Calvinist germ and coming out in some awful rash of rigidity and intolerance again. Now and then people talk of putting an end to the abuse, but it's as much the spectre of abuse as the spirit of liberalism they're paying for. Tolerance has to be abused in order for the masochist motives of liberals to be satisfied.

There's no secret about the tolerance of the Dutch.

Over the centuries they've let in Jews, Catholics, even Germans. There's a guilt thing here. That's why they still feel so uptight about the war. The Dutch are pragmatists. *Pragmatism pays.*

Morton's law applies. Morton's law states that benefactors are always beneficiaries.

Of course there are people who exploit the welfare system, but I'm not one of them. The exploiters apply for welfare as a second income, for which they don't have to work, in order to supplement the undeclared income for which they do.

I apply for welfare just in order to be.

Welfare has a significant advantage over wealth. Rich people, judging from some of the American relatives on my mother's side, have to look after their money. Wealth has fluctuations. One is worried it might become less, or one is greedy for it to become more. Having wealth means having certain projections into the future. One cannot be wholly engrossed by now. And so the rich person joins the rollercoaster of life like everyone else. The acute sensations of living now are confined to the moments of lift-off you feel in your stomach when the rollercoaster is down and about to go up or is up and about to go down.

But I don't have any expectation of going up or down. Living in a country that's as flat as a board, I have enough to get by on a level plane reaching to the horizon and far beyond. You could say my expectations are pretty stable. A thousand a month is pure now. On a thousand a month you're already into your basic Zen.

Welfare makes it possible to do without hope. Hope is another expression of anxiety. Deep down, hope is life denying the reality of death.

Life expectancy sets a standard to which everything else is adjusted. Insurance companies wouldn't have done much business in ancient Greece, because people expected to die this side of thirty. Old age hadn't been invented. Whereas villagers in the Caucasus these days find it worth while to quit smoking when they're a hundred years old and still going strong.

What if you lived for only a thousandth of the average span of life?

In this game, designed by my brother Morton, you're allowed to assume that everything is as it is, but lasts for only thirty days. Your diary will show you that ten or twelve generations ago, in January or February, the earth went through some kind of ice age. Amsterdam's canals were permanently frozen. Life in my condemned house, with almost no heating, would have been unimaginable.

Seasons? What the hell are they?

Alive for only thirty days in the summer month of July, I don't integrate these extremes as part of a recurring cycle of four seasons as I do within a life span lasting a thousand times longer.

Or what if you lived for a thousand times the average life span?

Everything is as it is, but lasts for seventy thousand years. Even weekend planning is of the order of aeons. Because I'll still be around, I pay as much attention to radioactive decay values of tens of thousands of years as I now do to the obvious consequences of leaving the kitchen stove on until some time next week. Difficult enough to do by accident. Who the fuck would leave it on deliberately?

Yet this is just what happens. Global stoves are deliberately left on. We can't handle that much future. The tiny time frame of our actions and the gigantic time frame of the consequences are completely out of kilter. Things are hotting up, in Vondeln Park and elsewhere. In the Alps, the glaciers are receding. In a hundred years they'll have melted altogether.

As an inhabitant of a perfectly level country, without

even the faintest rise of an expectation on my horizon, discounting the dykes that keep out the sea, I've been cultivating the art of Now, making notes towards a new definition of hope, that is, of hopelessness.

Once a global chemistry has got to work, the glaciers that have disappeared from the Alps and gone on strike with their melting colleagues at the poles may show up on the coast of Holland as walls of water a bit higher than the dykes. These could be expectations on someone's horizon, but not on mine.

Welfare brats like me don't think about the future. The value of having security is that you don't have to think about the future, but can afford to concentrate fully on now.

This is the first principle of hopelessness.

Don't think about the future.

The future holds no hope.

THREE

Listening to inner voices, broad-faced Pietje is the maid of bliss, a divine spy. She sits in a room full of people with a goofy smile and a look of absentmindedness on her face. Now and then she begins writing mysteriously on the pad on her knee, as if taking dictation from God. Everyone is used to her doing this, and pays no attention.

What does she write? Back-up copy, a ghostly paradigm of things, Morton called it, so that she has something when Now has gone and Then is lost. Talking to Erasmus, the gnome on her knee, Pietje does after her fashion what my brother and I used to do when we numbered things against the process of decay. We numbered things the way Pietje writes them down, to keep them from going away. To make them immortal, I guess. This is why Pietje, Mort and I once used to be so close.

It's Marion's birthday party.

Marion has twins inside her. Outside her, she wears a flimsy white maternity dress. The material stirs and billows, as if Marion were standing all the time beside an open window. Kristien is there in white, too, but without the open window effect. Kristien is tall and cool but her effect on people is essentially closed.

Breathed by a deep purpose that fills out every corner of her existence, Marion stands by her invisible open window and exhales joy. Why? She has paid a debt.

Marion is Pietje's friend. Somehow her parents survived deportation and the concentration camps. Marion was born in Amsterdam after the war, an only child among the very few Jewish children left. When the holocaust was gobbling up the Jews she'd not even been born, but her parents drip-fed into her the mentality of a survivor. She says the parents drip-fed into their daughter the guilt that survivors feel towards the people they've outlived. Now it was her turn *to make amends*. Marion must resurrect the dead and restore them to the living world. She must fill the gap left by the millions of the dead.

It's taken Marion all her life to find the man she wanted to have children by. How impatient the parents, how restless and neurotic the daughter became! How that gap she felt bound to fill must have weighed on her! Marion was getting older and thinner, and the gap she'd been told to fill grew wider and wider, until it became so wide it was no longer a gap but the empty horizon of Marion's life.

Marion stands exhaling joy in a white dress at her birthday party, because at this moment she's as far away from any thought of death as she'll ever be in her life. Marion's happiness is the image entirely filling her screen, an awareness of life so enlarged and sharply focused that for the moment she feels exempt from any claims of mortality.

'Marion, you're looking wonderful.'

'I *feel* wonderful!'

Conversation in the living-room is passed back and forth on trays. I take mine over to Kristien and we exchange.

'Hello, Kiddo. Still bumming around?'

'Still bumming around. Where did you get your lovely tan?'

'South Africa.'

'Oh? I thought one no longer went on holiday to South Africa.'

'One does again.'

'Are you still in convalescence?'

'Not exactly conva*les*cence. Just a holiday.'

'But you're not ex*act*ly back to work either, are you?'

'No. There are still days I'm so tired . . .'

One all.

For a moment I think of leaving it at that, but I'm irritated by the superiority in Kristien's manner. I want to do something to her to make her come down from her superior pedestal.

'The doctors must regard you as something of a medical phenomenon.'

'What d'you mean?'

Kristien looks at me warily.

'I mean, how is it possible to remain ill with glandular fever for five years?'

'They don't really know.'

'So they do. Regard you as.'

'There's nothing else they can do.'

'You know, my brother Morton . . .'

'Yes.'

'Mort had a pretty radical view about this. He thought that with illness it was basically the same as with things like personal hygiene or the state in which people choose to keep their teeth. He thought illness was your own responsibility.'

Kristien goes white under her tan.

'It's a monstrous view. It's wrong, and it's cruel.'

'I guess it was just Mort's personal view. He could never see himself as a victim. Morton always saw himself as the hero of his own life.'

'Well, that's not how *I* see it at all. Is it someone's fault if they're ill? I *do* see myself as a victim. I stand here and think: health, for God's sake. Why has everybody else got it but not me?'

'Maybe that's the attitude you have to change.'

13

'How?'

'You're not going to be well unless you think you can be.'

'All right. But how?'

'Something's gone absent. But maybe it's not health. Maybe it's something else that's missing, and you're ill because it's missing. Being ill *is* it's missing. That's what you have to find out.'

Kristien has regained her poise. Restored to coolness, she is no longer interested in finding anything out. We exchange a few more times, until there's nothing left, and we are handing each other empty trays.

'Have you tried the quiche?'

Gracefully, giraffe-like, her head above the tops of the trees, she lopes off to the buffet.

Pietje and I are already quarrelling on our way down the stairs.

'Why d'you have to be so stubborn, Pietje?'

'I'm not stubborn.'

'Yes you are.'

'I'm *not*.'

'You're always so fucking stubborn. I said I can take you on my bike and drop you off on the way.'

'Don't bother. I'll catch the tram.'

'I wasn't nasty to Kristien.'

'She was hurt nonetheless.'

'She was hurt by the truth.'

'How do you know? Do you *own* the truth? Do you have a monopoly on truth? You and your brother, oh-so-superior American boys teaching us dumb Dutch because you think you know it all better.'

'All that liberal crap. Scratch a Dutchman and you find a racist.'

'Don't you say that. Don't you *dare* say that.'

14

'I'm no more American than you are. My father's Dutch. I'm a Dutch citizen.'

We come out onto the street. Pietje stands fuming, her hands on her hips. On a large, slabby kind of woman like Pietje I admire shapely legs all the more for their unexpectedness.

'Take back what you said. I mean it, Kiddo.'

I look at her and jeer. 'There's your tram. Thought you said you were going to catch the tram.'

Pietje walks off. She ignores the tram. She just walks away. Pietje can be bloody-minded when she's stubborn.

We've lost the past, Morton wrote to me in his last letter. We no longer have any relations living there. The past is no longer the country from which we come. But Morton was obviously wrong about that.

Why was Marion having her babies? To please her parents with an act of atonement, an offering on an altar to the past.

Why was Pietje so stubborn? Because she didn't want the independence that had been forced on her by her parents' indifference. She wanted dependence as a measure of their love. Secretly, Pietje still wants her parents to come and kiss her goodnight.

And why did I always have to quarrel with her? Because of my emotional involvement with Pietje. The way I grew up, being involved with people was always through rows. In my family we *needed* rows. In my family we lived in a bazaar where people were buying and selling rows the whole time.

The past is still very much the country from which I come. I have *plenty* of relations living there. That's the whole trouble. Take me and my relations with my elder brother.

Just take me and Morton for a start.

FOUR

It's Christmas in the house that someone's lent us on Cape Cod. I'm six and Morton's ten. Morton and Dad are locked up in the room where the Christmas tree and the presents are waiting. They've already been in there three and a half hours. Moo, that's to say, my mother, and I are in various places – the kitchen, the bedroom, the bathroom, the hallway (where Moo is yelling at Dad through the door), a choice of locations that cater for her rising impatience whenever it needs more space to spill over. Tagging along, I have quite a stack of mixed feelings inside me.

These feelings are there throughout my childhood. There's a) the feeling of being *curious* whenever Morton's up to something I'm not in on, and b) the feeling of being *excluded* and warily *jealous* (the things that happen to Morton aren't always nice – electric shocks, painful falls from moving vehicles and high places), but this doesn't affect c) the terrific *admiration* for my hero, who holds me utterly in his thrall. Perhaps also worth mentioning is an instinctive feeling that because Morton is more Dad's boy and I am more Moo's, in terms of raw mother-share I for once have d) a slight advantage over my elder brother, which if necessary I shall exploit ruthlessly.

Dad and Morton have been in there for three and a half hours because they can't get the invention to work. The idea is to trip a light beam as we come in the door, activating Christmassy effects such as jingle bells, candles lighting up on the tree and a stream of confetti snow from a chute attached to the ceiling. Only yesterday the snow worked, perfectly. But today, this damn thing –

I ought to mention that Dad is an inventor. Inventing things is his job. My mother is sick to death of inventions. After two hours the Christmas lunch was spoiled, and now the Christmas has been, too.

'That boy is turning out just like his father,' Moo says, dragging a brush down through her hair and pulling it out – *sschzztk!* – with a wrench. I hear the sparks fly and, between the lines, my mother saying she's also sick to death of inventors. Between the lines I try to figure out if this means Moo is sick of *that boy*, too.

'OK,' bawls Dad gleefully from downstairs, 'ready!'

'You do what the fuck you like,' Moo bawls back, 'I'm not coming down.'

'Nor am I,' I second her from the top of the stairs in a prim little voice, cashing in the full benefit of my mother-share. At the bottom of the stairs Morton stands and fixes me with a look that makes me crumble. He has seen through me. Morton's look is not so much one of reproach as of deep sorrow for the cheapness of the betrayal.

This is the weight of Morton. Even when I am six my big brother represents a moral force beside which the dos and don'ts of my parents strike me as childish antics.

Sometimes Moo kind of *comes across* Morton. She can have a way of looking at her son as if she'd just discovered him for the first time in her life. 'That boy has to be seen to be believed,' she says at such moments. Already I sense

17

her estrangement. Moo sometimes acts like she's having to remind herself of her son. She calls him the Burning Bush. You can't miss him. Flame-headed, Morton stands around and seems to be on fire, as if the sun were just going down on him. He has this literally arresting colour.

'See that?'

'Wow!'

My big brother is a traffic light. He stops people in their tracks.

Inside a room, people look at Morton and think he's somehow lit up. You see them glance at the ceiling and try to figure out where it's coming from.

Actually, it's coming from inside him. The traffic-light hair pulls you up short, but even with that amazing colour people wouldn't look at him the way they do, not if Morton were just an ordinary kid.

My brother takes nothing for granted. If there's a different way, he'll try it. Using his left hand instead of his right, for example. Morton started switching to his left hand when he was four, Mother says, as a change from always doing things with his right. Now he's equally good with either hand. Left or right, he can also stand for an incredibly long time on one leg. Morton's been practising this for years in case he some day loses a leg.

Visitors on one of Morton's one-leg days are highly impressed by this feat, and as they watch him hopping around the house it's clear they suspect he might also be mentally defective. Alternatively, they come on a day when Morton is entering and leaving rooms only via the window, and Mother's forgotten the kind of things she often does at lunch, like the butter or the salt, and she says, 'Morton dear, would you fetch the salt?', and Morton takes off through the window, goes six floors down the fire escape, back up in the elevator, we hear the front door bell go and someone has to get up to let Morton into the apartment, and we wait another five minutes for him to show up with the salt at the window. On one of those days it's not Morton but my parents whom visitors look at as mentally defective, and you can see them wondering why we're all indulging this crazy little kid.

FIVE

The summer Morton goes to camp I work on the big tree on Cape Cod. The tree's an enormous oak, a monster of a climb. It's a real man-eater. For the past year I've stood on the ground and watched my brother swing up into the branches until he was lost in the green, man-eaten away out of sight.

'What's it like up there?' I call.

And Morton's shout comes down. 'Incredible! I mean just ha – ya – *maz*ing.'

'What's amazing?'

'These . . . like . . . they're impossible to describe.'

'What are impossible to describe?'

'I guess you could call them little . . . *peo*ple.'

'Little *people.*'

Frantically I hop around on the ground. I'm too small. I can't climb the tree.

'Morton?'

'Uh huh.'

'Can't you bring one of them down?'

'Jeeks, no! They'd *die.*'

Every day while Mort's away I'm working on the tree. I nail a couple of planks onto the trunk. I'm into the first branches. Then I'm into the green. I'm so scared I don't even think to look for the little people. When I'm past the scare I feel such triumph I don't particularly miss them, either. I can't wait for the day when Morton comes home to show him I can climb the tree.

While Morton's been away at camp he's learned how to juggle. He starts juggling the moment he gets off the bus. He can even do it with one hand. All the cousins visiting over the weekend crowd round to watch. There's this really neat blonde girl visiting whose name is Frederika. But Frederika's eight and she's two inches taller than me.

'Look at that!'

'Look everyone!'

'Wow!'

'Look at Morton!'

Later I get to show Morton how I'm able to climb the tree. Only it no longer seems like such a big deal. I mean, Morton makes a great big thing of it and is incredibly impressed, but the new juggling feat he's brought home with him kind of downgrades my tree.

It's hard to compete with the Burning Bush, always in the limelight, always the star.

I feel a kind of sediment sink to the bottom of the jar, a feeling you have when you give up on a longing deep down inside you. I imagine this is doom. Already I know that as long as Morton's around, Frederika's never going to be too interested in me.

SIX

It's my birthday in the apartment in Boston. I'm seven and Morton's eleven. Morton's just invented the heavenly rucksack.

We're eating cake with imaginary friends in the house of chairs and carpets Morton's built on top of my bed. Usually this house gets to be built on his bed. But Mort says I'm growing up and getting smart, and it's time the house was sponsored on mine. Everything is 'sponsored' right now. Sponsored is all the rage.

That reference to my getting smart. We just got back from visiting with Dutch relatives in Minnesota. When we go to see the Dutch relatives in Minnesota we travel on an overnight train. Every year there's the same argument about who sleeps on the top bunk. Every year Morton hijacks the argument his way.

'Listen, Kiddo. On the way to Minnesota *you* get to sleep on the bottom bunk. OK? And on the way *back* from Minnesota, *I* get to sleep on the top bunk. OK?'

Until I was seven I went along with this. I had an uncomfortable feeling there was something wrong with the deal, but I went along with it all the same.

We moved the birthday party into our bedroom after Dad arrived late, Moo said she could smell the other woman on him and slapped Dad across the face, Dad punched Moo in the face, and they both started rolling around on the floor, pulling out each other's hair.

When I see my parents do this kind of thing I get so desperate I pee in my pants. I start something I desperately want to try and stop and at the same time I know I can't. I'm sure this is pretty much how my parents must feel, because deep down my parents love each other.

Inside the chairs-and-carpets house on my bed I'm peeing in my pants and having a bit of a birthday snivel. Morton taps me on the shoulder and says, 'Happy birthday, Kiddo,' and hands me this invisible package. 'What is it?' I ask. 'Open it,' he says. Obediently I do.

'It's nice, Mort. Wow!'

Outside, my parents are still quarrelling. There's a loud bang as a door slams, and I hear my mother laugh.

'Hey, Mort.'

'Yeah?'

'What do I do with it?'

'Stupid-do! It's for keeping things you want to remember in. You carry it around with you all the time. OK, Kiddo. For the rest of your life.'

I stop crying. I'm intrigued. We're into the area of solemn pledges. I'm a sucker for solemn pledges.

'Like what kind of stuff d'you keep inside?'

'Well, if I were you . . . I mean, that Frederika girl, for instance. She liked you very much, Kiddo.'

'She did?'

'Isn't there something special you want to remember about Frederika?'

'Uh huh.'

'OK. So you put that inside. And how about Dad? Wasn't there something special you did with Dad that you'd like to put in too?'

'The day we went on the whale watch. It was foggy and stuff and everyone said we wouldn't see the whales even if they were there, but Dad had this whale-call thing in his pocket, and the whales came out of the fog right up beside the boat.'

'Put it in.'

'Can I put you in too, Mort?'

'Sure.'

'I want to put in what we're doing right now. This game we're playing.'

'It's not a game, Kiddo. It's for real.'

'What's it called? The thing we're putting all this stuff in.'

I'm pretty sure Morton made up the heavenly rucksack on the spur of the moment. Maybe it was just something to distract me while Moo and Dad were having their divorce row outside the bedroom door on my birthday. But maybe Morton had heard things I hadn't heard, and guessed what was coming even before that door slammed shut and we heard Mother laugh her skater-just-fell-through-the-ice laugh hysterically in the ensuing silence. The slam somehow went on echoing, even got into the heavenly rucksack, although it had no business echoing in there along with Frederika and the whales, and I can still hear it twenty years later, the sound of my father walking out on Moo and his family life.

SEVEN

So Dad got into the heavenly rucksack by the skin of his teeth and under false pretences, you could say. He went back to Amsterdam where it had all started with Moo, and I didn't miss him much and he didn't miss me, and in fact it was great not to play gladiator in an arena any more where people were taking swipes at each other, and even when you were still quite small you had to spend a lot of your time ducking. The trouble was that Morton went with him.

Parents have this idea they're there for the children and look after them, but it's an illusion. It's the other way round.

Without me, my high-grade hysteria mother would go off the rails. I *am* the rails. I give structure to a life that would otherwise lead nowhere. The question What is Life For is a ball that Moo can bounce off me and have come back with an answer. Life is for attending to Kiddo's material and spiritual needs. But what is Kiddo's life for?

Here's an open-and-shut case of a parent passing the buck. Because the question the parent's really asking is what is the parent's life for? The parent expects from the child an answer to this question. And boy, it had better be a *good* answer.

The question's never answered, of course. The buck just gets passed from one generation to the next. This is why parents and children mostly don't get along too well.

Morton and I were the alibis for the offences my parents committed in the name of marriage. It's crap about being born innocent. Morton and I were born into collusion and perjury. We bore false witness all the time, from the moment we opened our eyes and saw Mom and Dad taking swipes at each other and then kissing afterwards and pretending to make up.

I speak loosely of offences committed by parents. We're looking at a wide range here, from a minor misdemeanour such as withholding ice-creams at emotionally critical moments to a capital felony such as separating me and Morton.

Needless to say, it was Morton who initiated me, aged three and a half, into CAPCAA. This stands for Correct Assessment of Parental Claims versus Actual Achievements. Who gets the benefit, a) in the short term b) in the long run? Morton taught me that benefits can have *putative* and *actual* beneficiaries. According to Morton's law, the beneficiary often turns out to be the benefactor in disguise, and the benefit is often of a moral kind, involving considerable powers of blackmail and extortion. Morally superior benefactor feels entitled to turn on beneficiary, maybe years later, or to keep on turning, wearing the poor beneficiary down by moral erosion, the equivalent of the Chinese water-drip torture, repeating one single unanswerable charge: ungrateful! Every child is automatically exposed to the Chinese water-drip torture from the moment it's born.

When our parents announced the division of the spoils, that Dad would take Morton and Moo would take me, I knew there was no hope of appeal. Ideally, our parents should have gone their separate ways, and

Morton and I ours, if necessary in Minnesota. But Dad without Morton and Moo without me – both parents would quickly have gone to pieces. Both of them relied on their children for support.

So Dad and Morton went back to Amsterdam, because that was where Dad came from, Moo and I stayed in Boston, because that's where her folks were. For me and Morton these were the years of the Great Divide.

It was the first time we'd been separated in our lives. I didn't even see Morton for almost a year. I didn't see Frederika for almost two. And I never went on a whale-watch with Dad again. But all the memories that matter to me from the time before the Great Divide are stowed inside the heavenly rucksack Morton gave me so presciently on my seventh birthday, which I've carried around with me ever since.

After we saw Dad and Morton off at the airport I was having a snivel in the car when Moo, in a lunatic attempt to comfort me, said that it was all for the better as I would now be able to *step out of my elder brother's shadow.*

Of course it was the other way round. With Morton gone, no one there for me to check my facts on, my brother's shadow grew. The avatars of Morton proliferated. He'd been my hero, but now he became a legendary, a godlike figure.

Morton had seen to that. I'd have much preferred the proportions to be reversed, with Frederika, whales and others taking up seventeen-twentieths and Morton the remainder of the heavenly rucksack, but it's mostly my big brother I've carried around with me since.

EIGHT

Morton matriculates at Leiden University when he's sixteen, and goes on matriculating when he's dead, because I can't get him into the past tense. Engineering sciences are his major, I guess, but there's all this other stuff like Aramaic and Chinese, Zen and esoteric studies, piling up on the side. Morton's interests split clearly on a west-east axis, and I guess his personality sort of does that, too. There's the Morton you never really get to know, who has this merge-with-it-all thing. My education is pretty erratic, but wherever Mort's been able to have a hand in it, it's brilliant.

The summer I spend in Amsterdam, when I'm twelve, before Morton goes to Leiden, is billed as the end of the Great Divide. We stand looking at each other at Schiphol airport across a gap of five years in which I've stayed American and don't even know it, until I see how different my brother has become.

Maybe it shows up because I've stayed more like Moo. While I've been sliding around Florida in stretch limos, paid off with gigantic ice creams, an alibi to sleazy trade-offs between rich old farts who are trying to get into Moo's pants and Moo who is trying to get into rich old farts' bank accounts, Morton has been growing more like Dad, a connoisseur of things like resistors and capacitors who already filed his first patent when he was fifteen.

In some ways I stick with Moo. Both my parents were totally selfish people, with the difference that there was always a spare room for guests somewhere in Moo's selfishness, while Dad never had room for anyone but himself. Morton isn't like that at all. I mean, he's becoming more like Dad in some respects, but not in that way at all.

Dad has moved into this fall-down house off the Singel canal. It's a thousand years old or something, and it's a corner house, which in Amsterdam means a bummer. The higgledy-piggledy houses along the canals run this mutual support racket, propping their neighbours up, but corner houses aren't included in the scheme. Either they support themselves or they fall down.

At twelve, straight out of limos in Florida that are bigger than most people's apartments here, I take a fairly patronising attitude to a town I describe in a postcard home as a bunch of water full of dinky little houses that need trees screwed to the outside to keep them from falling down. It kills me the way the tourists goof around admiring this old trash and even stand back to get better pictures of it. Mort and I live at the top of a staircase that is so steep you can only get up into the roof on your hands and knees, with a pulley screwed to a beam outside to pull up your furniture afterwards. This isn't Swiss Family Robinson in your adventure section at Disneyland. No, this is where real people actually live. I mean, what a *dump*.

Lying in bed up in Morton's attic, I tell him about the alligators in the Miami sewers. I make them about twenty yards long, and arrange for one monster to come snarling up through the drains while Moo is in the bathroom having a pee. My brother says there aren't any alligators in Amsterdam and thinks it would liven up the neighbourhood to put a few in the canals. How do you *stand* it in this dump, I ask, and Morton is still

29

commiserating with me when I've bragged my way through my first homesickness and fallen asleep.

Morton is already dressed when I wake up next morning.

'Let's have breakfast,' he goes, while I'm still yawning in bed, opens the window and walks out.

'Hey!'

I jump out of bed and streak to the window in time to see my brother slide down a rope in a harness and sail through a second-storey window on the other side of the street.

'There's a string to draw the pulley back up whenever you're in shape to come down,' Morton calls, and I watch him go to the back of a room where people are sitting down to breakfast in the ordinary way that people do. What *is* this?

I come sailing down a minute later.

'Wow!'

'Hi. Sleep well? Howja like your eggs?'

Everyone in the room acts really offhand, like this is something completely ordinary. It's just how you do things here, Morton says, the way people call on their neighbours. Bullshit, I say, to be on the safe side. But five minutes later my dad comes zooming down through the window, too, followed by the old lady who lives in the basement of our house. I shut my mouth after that. I'm deeply impressed. I never say *dump* again.

The asshole kid from Alligatorland is conned by the dumbos in the dinky houses. Episode 1: Asshole kid has to eat humble pie. Morton's stunt with the pulley makes a first stab across the Great Divide.

I am twelve, and at the end of the day still game for pillow fights in the attic we share at the top of the fall-down house, just like we used to have. But Morton is sixteen now, with downy hair on his upper lip and a leery eye for the girls who shamble in and out of the disco-coffee-shop at the end of the street, and pillow fights are beginning to mean something different to him. Sometimes Dad will suddenly cut off the funny British English which is all I've ever heard him talk, and he and Morton start clearing their throats at each other in this really weird language. Morton's audio portrait in Dutch is a pretty worrying experience. I just don't recognise my brother, and I feel left out. Then there's the capacitor and resistor stuff going on in the background, way above my head, shit, I'm not *in*terested, and that's like another language, too.

Sometimes I look at Morton and say, hey, wait a minute, thought we guys were in this to*ge*ther, and Mort will snap out of it for a day or two and act his age, getting our Batman routine back together again, straight stuff that everyone agrees is fun, because one thing that hasn't changed is the way my brother can still read my mind. But gradually the doom sinks in. The Great Divide is there to stay. And because I'm twelve going on thirteen and have already eaten cratewise of the fruit of the tree of knowledge, my parents having dug it up and planted it in our back yard, watered it and manured it, when I was still a tiny little kid, I have a pretty clear idea of how me and my brother divide up. I am plain and Morton has knobs on, as Dad used to say, and Moo thought the same, although she put it differently. Now I love you dearly, as you know, but your brother *Mor*ton has class, Moo said, and whereabouts did that leave me?

Out of paradise, in retrospect, because life in America with Moo, Dad and Mort, whatever else it may have been, was pre-Divide, and so when Moo went and got married to the stretch limo in Florida, and Dad said I'd have to stay and go to school in Amsterdam instead, the result was that I didn't go back to America at the end of the summer, and somehow I've never got round to making the trip since. A guillotine came down and childhood ended, I mean, just like that.

31

NINE

Very gradually I sort of come to. I must have slept for a couple of hours. The afternoon has gone out of the room. You can tell by the light that it's getting on for evening. I wake up feeling lousy.

Laughter and voices come up from the street. I can identify Rick and Danny down there, and a couple of women, must be Danny's. They seem to be fooling around with a hose. The women shriek. Rick scolds Danny. Sounds like Danny is hosing down the women. Interesting. All the doors and windows and the hatch to the roof are open, but it's still too hot. I don't have the energy to get up and take a look.

I hear the front door shut and somebody trudging upstairs.

'Morton?'

He stops on the first landing, probably to see if he's got any mail. There's a postcard from a girlfriend in Spain, which I've read, and a couple of letters from institutes in the States.

'Kiddo? You in?'

'Bring up something cold to drink.'

It takes him ages to come up. Morton sounds somehow different on the stairs, as if he's put on weight.

When he comes in I'm lying on the mattress on the floor, doing a man dying of thirst in a desert. I drag my way to a water hole. Morton comes in wearing a Peruvian cap with ear-flaps. He doesn't take much notice of me dying of thirst. I have to remind him.

'. . . water . . . water . . .'

'Oh, sorry. I forgot.'

Clutching my throat, I expire in agony. There's a resounding splash in the street below, followed by more shrieking of women. Morton steps over my dead body and goes to the window. He stands there looking down and says in Dutch, 'I feel sorry for Rick.'

In English he goes on, 'All the humiliations he has to endure on Danny's account.'

'That's Danny's pound of flesh, his price for sucking Rick's cock.'

'There's more to it than the sex. He's a human being and he hurts. Rick loves Danny. He doesn't want to lose him.'

I prop myself up on one elbow and look at my brother in his Peruvian cap with the ear-flaps.

'Love is a deal just like anything else. Rick keeps Danny and allows Danny his women in return for having Danny around as an object of love, or sex, or whatever. They've done a deal, Mort. Aren't you hot wearing that thing?'

'No, actually, I'm not. Don't you have any ideals?'

'For example, love is *not* a deal like anything else? I don't trust that stuff with ideals. I think it all breaks down to something else. Self-interest is always the bottom line.'

'You've become too cynical, Kiddo. Have you and Hella had a fight? Or is it something between you and Dad?'

'Miaow.'

'OK.'

Morton falls back on the sofa, pulls his shoes off with

his toes and hangs his legs out of the window. I watch him take the postcard and the two letters out of his pocket, interested to see – he's pernickety about his letters – how he'll respond to the choice of ripping the letters open or getting up again to fetch a paper knife. He's already anticipated this, however, and chosen another alternative, which was to open the letters downstairs. He just takes a peek inside the two letters and then drops them on the floor. He props the card up on his chest and says nothing for such a long time that I think he must have dozed off.

'Remember a girl called Frederika?'

'You bet.'

'She's married and has a kid. Mensje met her in Spain. She says Frederika sends her love to both of us.'

I already read the postcard a couple of weeks ago, plenty of time to remember Frederika. Rummaging in the heavenly rucksack, I've been admiring her again under the giant tree on Cape Cod, with her long blonde hair, in those pre-Divide summers when Morton and I used to travel on the overnight train to stay with the relatives in Minnesota, and Moo stood on the platform, waving goodbye, until you couldn't see her any more.

'Frederika must be going on seventeen or eighteen.'

'Eighteen and a half.'

'And a half, huh?'

Morton turns and looks at me.

'So what's the bottom line on Frederika, Kiddo? How does Frederika break down?'

I don't have an answer to this. All I have is a slight ache. Voices and laughter, the clink of glasses and clatter of plates, come flocking up from the street. The evening sun is shining through the attic window. I watch a fly on hold under the ceiling, roaming in a wide circle, lighting up when it passes through the sunbeam and its wings reflect the light.

I change the subject.

'Finished at Leiden?'

'Pretty much. I cleared my locker at the lab and brought the last of my stuff back today. Although . . .'

'You got your doctorate? They actually hand something over?'

'Oh, sure. I mean . . .'

Morton throws up his hands.

'In fact they'd quite like me to stay on. Research work. That kind of thing.'

'And those letters from Johns Hopkins and MIT?'

He yawns, not too convincingly.

'They're offering me research posts, too.'

'That's great, Mort. That's fantastic.'

'Well, there was the old Boston angle I actually had in mind, but . . . I don't know. Maybe it's not an angle any more.'

'I guess not.'

Morton holds the ear-flaps out sideways from his head.

'How about you?'

'I've quit school.'

'Dad said.'

Morton takes a nibble at a fingernail.

'And?'

'The world is my oyster. I'm checking it out. There are lots of things going on in the oyster that not even you knows anything about.'

'Know. For example?'

'Here are just some of the options.'

I put my hands behind my head and read the list off the ceiling.

'Trainee applicant in warehouse management in Rotterdam. Interesting openings in the fruit picking industry in South Africa. A challenging career with North Sea fisheries. It's gripping stuff.'

Down in the street I hear Rick calling my name. Morton gets up and leans out of the window.

'Yeah?'

'It's Danny's birthday, guys. Won't you put on your bathing costumes and come down and join us?'

'Sure. We'll be down. Thanks, Rick.'

Morton takes off the Peruvian cap and puts it on the plaster head of Queen Victoria on the shelf. He sits down cross-legged on the floor, fishes a tobacco pouch out of his pocket and rolls a cigarette.

I watch the high-altitude fly that's been on hold under the ceiling begin to meander lazily down, taking a couple of turns around Morton's head, and I listen to that warm chorus of people you get around the middle of a meal, rising bright and steady from the street below. The stifling heat in the attic seems to have dulled the edge of my feelings, because when I think of Frederika, Moo, an expanse of North Sea fisheries reaching grey and level to the horizon, all I have is a slight ache. I'm concentrating on the deep glass ashtray that Morton keeps turning between his fingertips, so when he says, 'I mean why, Kiddo, you had pretty good grades?' I guess my mind is more on watching that fly come cruising in to take a sniff at the ashtray than on Morton or his question.

There's no honest answer to the question. There's no honest *thinking* about it even, not with Morton and his homing devices around. My elder brother has always been the winner who takes all, but the subject of envy is absolutely taboo between us. We don't talk about it, because envy officially doesn't exist. Morton may have his suspicions, yet if there's one thing I feel bound to do, as much for myself as for my brother, it's to keep him from having too close a look at the envy I've got bottled up inside. Envy is a grubby feeling. I imagine it being served up on a plate, stained a dirty brownish sort of colour. It's one of the more shameful feelings that can hang around. So long as I keep clear of Morton's orbit and the comparisons aren't showing me up, OK, I can for*get* about envy, but here and there the doom spot will soak through, absolutely it will, like the bloodstain in the horror movie.

Take this business about Frederika with a kid at eighteen and a half, and Morton with a doctorate in engineering at twenty. It hits me with a feeling of *panic*. It makes me feel I want to pee in my pants. Why am I still sitting around in a classroom, wasting time just being average? Quitting school makes better sense. I feel I'm losing all these people who matter to me to a whole lot of changes I no longer have anything to do with. Other people are making the rules, and somehow I've got left behind. Suddenly I'm no longer part of the game. My life is beginning to be over before anything much to speak of has happened.

This isn't passing through my mind at the time, however, or not exactly. Mentally I keep off the subject. Fortunately it's too hot in any case. Instead I look at Queen Victoria in her Peruvian cap and make conversation.

'Did Dad mention he got married?'

'No. When'd he get married?'

'At the end of last week. Thursday or Friday, I'm not sure. I didn't hear about it until afterwards. Would you roll me a cigarette?'

Morton takes out his pouch.

'So what happened?'

'Dad and Helen left the house at eleven, got married and back to the house in time for lunch. I happened to be sunbathing on the roof and saw them leave on their bicycles. When Helen called and I came down for lunch Dad told me he and Helen had just got married, and handed me a small glass of sherry for a toast. I mean,

Jesus. I put the small glass of sherry down and walked out of the house. I've not spoken to him since.'

Morton taps the cigarette against a box of matches, lights it and passes it over.

'But you know Dad. He does things on the spur of the moment.'

'What d'you mean, *things*.' I spit out bits of tobacco. I'm in a mean mood. 'Dad is an asshole on the spur of the moment. You can't get married on the spur of the moment. Maybe in Florida you can, but in Holland you can't. You need registrars and forms and stuff. You have to apply in advance. He went sneaking off to his wedding while I waved from the fucking roof. He went and got married behind my back.'

'Who has a problem here, you or Dad?'

'Oh come on. Don't give me that crap.'

'You need the self-pity? You've got to have a crutch? Who do you want to make responsible for your life?'

'Fuck *off*, will you.'

'What's in it for Dad? What are you doing for *his* motivation? Dropping out of school?'

'It's all very well for you, Mort. You're the genius. You're everybody's golden boy. You can afford to preach. Dad doesn't give a shit about me. He doesn't care if I'm in school or out of school, or on the moon, he wouldn't even notice, and *that's* the problem.'

The moment I blurt this out I'm wishing I could unsay it. I've broken the taboo. The boil bursts, and a lifelong reproach comes rushing out. Something happens to my brother, I mean, im*med*iately. The freckles turn so pale it's like they disappeared from his face. It's like we reached the edge of a cliff, and this time I've taken him over with me. Morton is plummeting like a stone. There's a long silence through which I can hear my brother fall. It's *eer*ie. I feel I've done something unforgivable. Suddenly I want to touch him, but the

38

only gesture I can make sort of in Morton's direction is to reach over and stub out my cigarette in the ashtray lying beside him.

After a while I pretend to stretch, and I go, 'Jesus it's hot.' I clear my throat, like something was stuck in it. 'Aren't you hot? Mort?'

Morton is lying on the floor with his chin in his hands, looking down into the ashtray where I've just stubbed out my cigarette. The fly I've been tracking all afternoon takes off one more time, hovering drowsily around inside the ashtray.

Mort says, 'Do you sometimes still miss Moo?'

Table noises, talk and laughter, come up in bursts from the street below.

'Sometimes.'

'If you had the choice, what would you choose? The pain you feel when you miss something that was there, or the pain you feel because it never was?'

'How d'you mean?'

'To have been close to Moo and miss her when she's gone, or not to miss her, and for that to hurt, because it means you'd never been close to her?'

I sit in the attic facing Morton. I really try to concentrate on his question, but it's hot and I'm thirsty. I say, 'That's a tough question, Mort', to show him I'm giving it my attention, and I try to imagine these different pains he's talking about, and I can't. I feel depressed. Down in the street it has suddenly gone quiet, and in the attic it's beginning to get dark.

Mort is still lying on the floor with his chin in his hands. He has his head right over the ashtray and is staring into it. 'Hear it?' he asks, without looking up.

'Hear what?'

'A sort of papery, rustling sound.'

I listen, but I can't hear anything.

'No. What is it?'

'It's cigarette ash scattering under a fly's wings. It's ploughing a furrow in the ash with the whir of its wings. It's one of those day-flies, and you can see its day is ending. You can hear it.'

'I can't.'

'You're too far away.'

We sit in silence for a while longer, until it's dark and I'm beginning to get restless. There's a shout from the street.

'Hey, you cocksuckers! When are you coming down?'

It's Rick yelling again, giggling, drunk.

'Guess we'll have to,' I say, and Morton makes a move at last. He gets to his feet and together we go down.

People are sitting on benches in the street, and at one end of a bench there's a girl sitting with crossed legs whom we notice immediately, because she's sitting there with a notebook on her knee, her face turned a little away from the others, sort of eavesdropping, as if she were waiting for dictation, but not from anybody here, from someone she can hear talking somewhere else.

This is our first view of Pietje, and Morton and I set eyes on her at the same moment.

TEN

It's five in the morning and we're onto the subject of musical instruments. Pietje pedals evenly at a strong, steady pace.

'There's a room near the Concertgebouw which is full of pianos. Pianists go there before the concerts to choose the instrument they want to play. There they stand, all those sleekly lacquered, black grand pianos. You want to stroke them. They're not like things at all. It's like being in a stable surrounded by racehorses, about to explode into sound.'

This is nice and old-fashioned, seeing a girl home. Mort and I have seen girls home together before, but it was never as much fun as this. At five in the morning we're in need of an outing. We're feeling pretty frisky and racehorsey ourselves. On the approach to the hump-backed bridge we fan out and close in again on the other side, freewheeling. We take Pietje in the middle. On either side of her we dart off, working in the twirls and showmanship and all that stuff, but Pietje's where we take our bearings. We're always keeping her in the middle.

'I mean, pianos are alive, aren't they.'

This is so obvious it doesn't need saying. It's so damn

obvious that pianos are alive and kicking and just raring to go that Mort and I whoop and swerve, putting in an optional slalom round a few lamp-posts for good measure. Already at eighteen Pietje pedals strong and steady, without frolics, surging straight ahead, like a freighter that's moved up out of the canal and onto the sidewalk. But she laughs after she says this, sprawling and breathy, and you can hear the exhilaration in the sound she makes.

'You know, Stradivari—'

Ho ho! – Pietje fires her big canon, squashing Mort's bid to get into the conversation – Ho ho!

'Stradivari used to keep his violins in—'

Mort reappears, edging back in after a manoeuvre round a trash-collecting truck.

'In his bedroom before they were varnished. In a corner, under the bed, wherever. Imagine those *sexy little violins* resting in the master bedroom, their por— porches is what I'd like to say although I mean their pores, open and sort of acquiescent . . .'

'Whuuh!'

'. . . Eavesdropping after a fashion. Stradivari seems to have thought some kind of transference took place, of certain bedroom . . . er, emanations, which got absorbed into the grain. Quite what Mrs Stradivari felt about—'

'She was jealous.'

'She was?'

'I know she was.'

Take as given. Pietje was there two hundred years ago, Erasmus on her knee, taking it all down as she listened smiling to Mrs Stradivari's confidences in Cremona.

Pietje comes across in some of the things she says with the same unsinkable certainty you sense when you see the way she rides her bicycle. But there's also this other Pietje whom Mort and I see. This big girl who can seem so placid inside her unsinkable certainty has also something waiflike that makes Mort and me want to take her in the middle to protect her from all those encircling predators.

We hit a patch of rough cobbles and begin to clatter, all three of us, only Mort and I rise out of the saddle while Pietje, more generously padded, remains sitting. With admiration we watch the way her natural shock-absorbers handle the bumps. With sidelong glances we take the measure of it. We appreciate the size and grace of the operation. Pietje has tanker in her genes. Once in motion she'll need half a mile of water to come to a standstill. Meanwhile Mort and I keep shooting off at tangents and doing all this fancy stuff, showing her what aces we are on our bikes. We are the lady's figure-skaters. And she's loving it. Lady's face has been bliss all the way from the party.

'Maybe there's a hidden passage between animate and inanimate things.'

'Carbon atoms.'

'Maybe Stradivari found it.'

'Tapped it. The carbon atoms in the pores –'

'A porous passage –'

'A norous, nor worse, northwest passage –'

'Whuu-u-uh!'

Morton and Pietje are shouting this stuff across the street at full pelt on their bicycles. Jubilant in a cloud of luminous certainty, I can feel the idiot grin on my face. No question about it – as we cycle down the long straight stretch of the Keizersgracht between Westerkerk and Leidse Plein we are unlocking the mysteries of the universe.

Under the trees along the canal the morning opens an avenue of shadows. Early morning light, stalling, still hangs there heavily like a green awning. Shutter barks up at an overhead window. Bird puts down its skids, landing on a furrow of water. A tram is crossing the canal ahead,

43

a car roars up from behind and we scatter, converge and take Pietje in the middle again. The air streams against our faces, behind her Pietje's long brown hair floats downstream on the wind, locked into the corners of one another's eyes we feel ourselves flow down the same stream into the same green morning that is opening up around us.

ELEVEN

Vacation time comes along, and Pietje wants us to meet her friend Anna, whose parents have a place by the sea. The four of us find ourselves in this two-bedroomed cottage right on the edge of the coastal mud-flats called the *waddenzee*, Anna, Pietje, Morton and me. I don't have to delve into the heavenly rucksack to get this stuff together. I can haul it out by the reel.

Clips from day one show a bronzed blonde Amazon splashing naked into the creek. We're hardly out of the car and Anna has her clothes off. Mort and I have no choice but to watch. I mean, we're not kids, seen it all before and it's no big deal.

OK – we're totally agog. Streaking through the water, this bounding body of Anna's puts together a really stunning package. Pricks perk up in shorts and say Hey, take a look at *that*. It's the kind of happiness they dream of inside their shorts but don't believe will ever happen.

Dividing two by four, my brother and I end up sharing the other bedroom. It's an OK arrangement. But when lights are out and one starts thinking about alternative bedroom-sharing arrangements, certainly I do, it seems an awful waste.

'Guess people *would* get quite a tan up here on the

coast,' goes Morton in the dark, and from that it's clear he's headed the same way. Both of us are virgins, but Mort is more uncomfortable than I am when the subject turns to sex. He's not the kind of guy who exclaims 'What mouth-watering tits!' or 'What a smurfy little arse!' Instead he goes on about people and tans, and the fact that he says people *would* get quite a tan is Morton's way of letting on he's been giving the matter some thought, and that this Anna has him really sexed up.

Next day, the rest of us start working on our tans, too.

My brother in the nude – I'm used to it, but other people aren't. I have to make a conscious effort to see this through their eyes. Mort on the outside is as interestingly equipped as he is on the inside. The girls pretend to look the other way, but they don't fool me. It's not the size. Not just the size. It's the angle. When you watch Mort coming along the beach you feel an urge to put your head on one side – the sort of urge you feel when you see a picture hanging crooked on a wall, and you're tempted to tweak it straight. Because this thing is lopsided as hell. It defies gravity. What Morton wears out there in front is a hanging tower of Pisa.

It's not long before the first jokes are being cracked, which tends to have a deflationary effect. The sexiness that was building up nicely starts building down again. Still, when the lights are out and we lie in bed we're both busy editing the day's video.

'You know when Anna was lying on the sand, and Pietje poured that can of cold Coke over her back, and she—'

'Yeah.'

'How did that look from your angle, Mort?'

'Looked pretty good.'

'Got a whole load of Coke over her tits, too, and then she lay them down in the sand again. So when, later, she got them *up*, there must have been quite a lot of sand sticking . . . that's the bit I missed. How did that clip end? Did you happen to check it out?'

'Don't think I did. I must already have gone up from the creek to fix lunch. Right . . . Pietje and I were in the house.'

'Pietje? I thought she'd gone shopping.'

'She'd just got back. So we fixed lunch together and hung around talking in the house.'

'Oh?'

I miss a beat.

'What were you talking about?'

'Seemed to us you and Anna were hitting it off. We thought we'd leave you to it for a while.'

My suspicions are alerted by this show of considerateness. What's this *we* and *us* Morton's talking about? It dawns on me that while I've been posted up the creek, lolling beside Anna and getting an eyeful of the Body, my brother has sneaked past in a flanking manoeuvre. I can hear him grinning there in the dark.

During editing sessions we've tended to avoid talking about Pietje, as if she wasn't in the video at all. Instead we've been throwing each other dummy passes, egging each other on, using these lurid cartoons of Anna as a decoy. I misread what Mort was visualising under the tan. It's not the Body who has him sexed up. It's Pietje.

The weather breaks and for days it rains. I never used to notice the weather, but now I find I'm paying attention to it. Suddenly it's there, hanging morosely around the house along with a lot of other stuff that never used to bother me. The rain taps at the window and I look up, half expecting to see the careers officer looking in to finalise the option on North Sea fisheries. I'd like to tell him to go away, but I know he won't. I'm becoming a weatherbound adult like everyone else. The only solution is to postpone, to wait for the weather to improve.

47

Meanwhile the wind goes howling around the house, and it seems unbelievable that only a couple of days ago we were out sunning by the creek with nothing on. We play a lot of games and walk for miles over the *waddenzee*, rain capes billowing, leaning into the wind. This looks pretty scenic in the video, but it's not an awful lot of fun. There's a new routine of smoke in the downstairs rooms and a smell of damp clothes drying all over the house. Everything is muffled by damp clothes. The zip of the first week sort of leaks away.

Then the phone rings and Anna suddenly has to leave for Amsterdam. At least, we assume it rings, because Mort and I are out collecting firewood at the time and when we get back to the house and Pietje tells us, Anna has already gone.

The footage for the next two weeks comes frame by frame, reluctant to move on. It's so slow motion it's more a series of stills. Pietje has the stage to herself. This time, when she unwraps, her body emerges against a background of rain capes and layers of clothes. It makes her nakedness seem vulnerable, somehow much more exciting. We're into the warm weather again, camping by the creek, soft drinks cooling in the water, tuna sandwiches curling at the edges in the sun. This time there's no Anna alongside to distract. It's like starting from scratch, getting to know Pietje all over again.

Spending most of our time lying outside on the ground, we begin to feel a lot closer to the sky. There's a stronger sense of gravity pushing you down against the ground, but you look up and all you see is sky. There comes a moment when you leave gravity behind you and start to float. Above and below, the opposites graze each other without colliding. You feel good in the balance. Pietje calls this harmony. We do what Pietje calls harmony exercises. My brother Morton is there on the other side, with Pietje in the middle. Lying on our backs, we distribute gravity evenly all over our bodies and compare how it otherwise feels when all that pressure's stacked on two small feet. I have this dream of Pietje, Mort and me lying on inflatable mattresses and floating down the canals of Amsterdam. We are instructors in a municipal harmony exercise, and the banks of the canal are lined with cheering spectators throughout the city. The Queen of Holland, in an enormous floral hat, receives us in her lap and hands out harmony awards.

During the day we hear the running water of the stream, and as we lie by the creek doing our harmony exercises we are floating down with it. Not actually, although it feels as if we were. We lie suspended somewhere between the ground and the sky. The sense of slow motion has to do with the sense of weightlessness and a presence of sky that excludes everything else. Walking along the *waddenzee* is like balancing on a narrow margin at the edge of this enormous sky. After a while you feel yourself beginning to merge. Pietje says to imagine our shoulder blades are sprouting legs and walking us across the *waddenzee* on our backs.

Morton and I think this is hilarious. Pietje doesn't laugh. She takes herself seriously to a fault. Perhaps this is why she seems vulnerable. The bare coastline with the cottage hanging in at the edge seems so much Pietje's landscape. Pietje in the middle is sometimes isolated by our laughter.

After three weeks in the cottage it's time to go back to Amsterdam. We're sitting at the supper table on our last evening. Pietje makes a confession.

'Anna and I had a row. That's why she left. There wasn't a phone call at all.'

'What was the row about?'

'Anna's very jealous. Usually boys go for *her*, you

know. But neither of you did, and she felt ignored. She felt she was outside the circle.'

'What circle?'

'The circle that formed the night we met at Danny's party. Anna stood outside that circle.'

Pietje gets up and clears the rest of the things off the table.

'I watched both of you looking at Anna in a way you didn't look at me. I wondered which of you would be drawn to Anna, and step outside the circle. I thought one of you would prefer Anna. How should I choose between you? One of you would go, and then fate would decide.'

Pietje, the house sphinx, says this with an absent-minded smile that doesn't have anything to do with what she's talking about. What does Pietje's smile mean?

She comes and sits between us at the table. She looks down at the table and sweeps crumbs together with her fingers into a heap beneath the palm of her hand. We *all* start taking a closer look at the table, which now seems kind of empty, with Pietje's fingers ferreting around in the emptiness of the table like some little night animal that's come out to feed. We're all sitting there leaning on the table. We're leaning into this emptiness of table where the three weeks suddenly seem to have gone, and all that's left is Pietje's hand, a table-hog rooting around in the middle for the crumbs.

She opens her fist, and a coin is mysteriously lying in her palm.

'Heads or tails?'

'Tails!' says Morton in a flash.

She spins the coin.

It hovers for a moment, wandering jerkily with little bursts of speed across the table. Then it stays put and rocks up and down on its rim for an agonisingly long time, like it's humming and hawing and can't make up its mind. I watch that coin teetering around on the table, a doom taking shape with me and Morton in the balance, and suddenly I panic. I want out of this. I'm up and running across the *waddenzee* before that coin delivers my doom.

I run about half a mile before I fall in a muddy hole and think this thing through. Maybe I overreacted. I realise it's not so much I'm worried about losing, it's more like I'm scared of winning. This could be the problem I have in life. I reflect that it's not too friendly out on the *waddenzee* at night without a moon. It's dark as hell out here. If they turn out the cottage lights I'm never going to find my way back. I'll be cut off by the tide and drown. The mud-flats on the North Sea coast are such a vast, empty place and the hinterland is so flat that people are sometimes found wandering round the tideland who've lost their way and gone mad. I can make out a small beam behind me in the dark and I turn back with relief, sloshing my way home.

The light in the living-room is burning, making a dim splash on the stairs. I sneak up. Pietje's door is open but the light is out. I whisper 'Pietje?' There's no answer. I go into the room opposite, where Mort's already asleep. I'm a little hurt to find them both asleep while I'm still out on the *waddenzee* in mortal danger, for all they know, lying in some muddy hole with a sprained ankle and the tide about to come in. I imagine Mort and Pietje coming down to breakfast and finding my corpse washed up in the creek. I'm already getting into some interesting funeral arrangements, with Led Zeppelin playing beside my coffin on a black barge piled with mourners' wreaths and floating down the canals by special permission of the Bridge, Sluice & Harbour Fee Authorities, when I drift off elsewhere for what seems to be just a few seconds, and I feel something tickling my stomach. I haven't woken up but started to dream. It's a nice dream. It's a *hell*uva nice dream. I lie there and let this thing happen, the warm, moist feeling of my dick inside Pietje's mouth. It's Pietje's hair tickling my stomach, it's her head my fingers reach up and touch because this dream is happening for real. From the amount of squirming going on around me I get the impression that me with my dick inside Pietje's mouth is not the only thing happening in this bed. I hear the little huffing snorts that give him away, the kind of noise my brother makes when he's run up the stairs from the basement to the attic, and I know that Morton's in on this, badgering at the other end, with Pietje in the middle, grinning at me in the dark. It's like Pietje's on a see-saw going up and coming down on me at one end with Morton rocking her backside at the other. I can see this video in the dark and it's really turning me on. Morton's rocking and Pietje's see-sawing and getting her teeth into me every time she comes back down, and Jesus I *am* drowning, I can hear Pietje panting and Morton giving this funny little sigh as we sort of all fall down. It's hysterical, I don't know why, but the first thought that comes dancing through my head is *you made it, Kiddo,* and I start laughing like an idiot, thinking this is a toss that divides down the middle, heads *and* tails, because Mort and I just made it with Pietje in the middle. There are neon signs winking Adults Only and Welcome to the Club around us in the night, and they're still flashing on and off in my head when the three of us stand shivering naked outside the cottage and run into the dawn, chasing each other along the creek and splashing through the stream while the light comes up over the rim of the sky, and flings out at us the gigantic carpet of the shore.

TWELVE

The view of the world which Morton tries to share with me in the attic of the corner house lacks any certainty at all. I guess it's pretty sophisticated stuff, but Morton drops names like Heisenberg, Gödel and Mandelbrot in a conversational way like these guys lived on the block and were our pals in the Singel neighbourhood gang. During vacations, when he's back from Leiden, Morton has them in most nights, and I get used to them hanging around. I don't understand stuff like Heisenberg's uncertainty principle or Prigogine's dissipative structures, or what they're for, but I do know they're there and Morton can explain to me in roughly what direction they're headed. Most people haven't even heard of them.

I guess it doesn't matter if you haven't, because a gist is all we get. The view is not precise. It's blurred. In fact the view of the world is blurred so much that it disappears behind the views of its parts.

Some of Morton's drawings hang on the attic wall. An engineer's drawings show this dissolution of an object into its components. It looks like the object is being blown apart. Take the diagrams of an electric shaver you see in the instructions for use and maintenance. The detachable head of the shaver is zooming up, the base

53

drops away, the batteries and screws and other components are streaming away to the edges like they're responding to a centrifugal force. You can keep on exploding parts until eventually you lose sight of the shaver altogether.

Mort says scientists do the same thing with time. Events begin and cease to happen within millionths of seconds.

When time starts imploding this way the present gets incredibly dense. You get this incredibly dense quality of present time. There's no time for anything else. Past and future stream out to the edges, and eventually you lose sight of them altogether.

What is a thing? Morton has this question very much on his mind at the time. He's tracking the paradox that if a thing can be divided into an infinite number of parts, then the thing must itself be infinite. Mort says this is a famous paradox. An old Greek guy thought it up a couple of thousand years back. Morton's law is going to show that the proliferation of parts is proportionate to the diminution of the whole. In other words, the more parts you get, the less whole.

I'm not the best partner for Morton's games of tossing ideas around, but I do my best because I know how much they matter to him and that he wants to be able to share them with me. I am another onlooker and I have a different point of view. My point of view is not so much what Morton's telling me about these ideas as what these ideas are telling me about Morton.

The guy who talks this way about hyper-acceleration inside an infinitely expanding present is still the same guy who gave me a heavenly rucksack for my seventh birthday. Instinctively I sense that Morton is going to be in trouble here. This brother of mine who has a penchant for Peruvian-style caps with ear-flaps has very poor screening-out facilities. His thin, freckled skin is highly porous material. Morton is a walking, talking, ten-fingered case of osmosis, and everything comes aboard.

I give up on the vacancies the career officer has been keeping open with warehouse management and North Sea fisheries. I become a bartender at Siberia instead. Pietje's working in a bar, too. Siberia is where we all meet. Morton is kind of killing time before going off to America and making his great discovery. Meanwhile he's polishing his patents and giving our dad a little help with a salt-water conversion machine he's been working on not too successfully since about the time I was born.

It's through Morton I get to know Harko. Morton meets him first, and later I kind of inherit him. It's pathetic. I even get my friends from Morton. The two of them meet at Siberia, where Harko shows up after a month on an oil rig with his pockets full of money and takes a shine to Morton, and Morton to Harko, and together they blow a couple of thousand guilders in a single night. It's one of those fuel-burning friendships that starts at full blast and instantly rockets sky-high.

Harko's dad is an airforce pilot who's grounded at forty, goes into early retirement a couple of years later and within a week is a full-time alcoholic. There's always been a lot of booze around the NATO bases where the family is stationed, but with the prospect of clambering into the cockpit on Monday morning on low-flying missions a hundred yards above the ground at something like a thousand kilometres an hour Harko's dad is able to handle the alcohol and has always dried out by Sunday night.

His son sneaks upstairs to try on Mummy's bras and knickers and take a swig from the emergency bottle hidden in the bedroom cupboard while the old folks are watching telly. Risk addiction runs in the family. It's not so much the kinky stuff and the booze that turns Harko on as the risk of being found out.

Harko quits working on rigs and gets a regular job with Shell. He invents this doppelgänger life. From nine to five he wears a suit and tie and works in an office, evenings and weekends he hangs out on the trash heap with whores and junkies. It's not just the different gear, the people and the environment. Harko has two different personalities. He's a controlled schizophrenic. Being sick, in Harko's case, is a kind of health. It's what enables him to function as a normal person for the other half of the time.

Morton has never met anyone like Harko. For my brother, Harko's life is like an accelerator track in which high-speed particles collide and leave imprints of forms of matter which elsewhere are not visible, not in Morton's experience of life. Morton is fascinated by Harko. Because no one questions Morton. He's the guy with doctorates in physics and engineering from Leiden University by the age of twenty. Right now he may be hanging round bars with Harko, but everyone knows he's going places. There's this logo on Morton's cap. At twenty my brother is a genius.

He usually shows up in Siberia around ten o'clock. Mort's not much of a talker. He only really talks with me. He helps a conversation along by the way he's able to listen. Here and there he gives it a prod, and it shambles off, like a vagrant given a destination. People talk an awful lot in Siberia and don't know where they're headed. They appreciate having Mort around to prod their conversations because he can make everyone sound smarter than they are, and all that talk seems to get licked into shape. Probably they don't even notice Morton's habit of glancing down and to one side. This means he's checking the configurations of a problem and will have them all at his fingertips when he looks up again a few seconds later. It's a habit he's acquired playing chess with himself, and to me it always seems like

56

someone just tiptoed up behind him and whispered the score.

Meanwhile he's waiting. It can only be Pietje he's waiting for. She doesn't get in until around midnight when I finish work, and then Morton and I usually see Pietje home.

There's Pietje in the middle, and maybe this is why I feel closer to my big brother than at any time in my life. With Pietje between us, I feel equal for the first time. Triangular's not the word for a thing without corners. This is smooth and round, a perfectly circular relationship. Mort and I flow in the same stream, parting and closing around Pietje in the middle.

She has the habit of just taking off and disappearing without saying a word. This time she's been out in Steenhoven at her parents' place for a week. She comes back with a new fad about not turning on any lights in her room. She says she likes it better when we lie there together in the dark. Pietje wants it that way. Her room is always dark.

We come and go in darkness. In late August nights the yellow lamps along the canals blur when mist rises off the water, and you can see the light crumbling at the edges. It's a sign the fall is coming.

Someone I can't see is coming up behind Morton and whispering in his ear. He talks about going to America. He talks about leaving home. He wonders why Pietje no longer turns the light on in her room.

The engineering drawings Morton pins up along the attic walls are getting more and more complicated. He says parts keep on imploding and forming new clusters of parts, and these implode in turn. I guess Morton's in trouble with his invention. Lying in bed reading comics, I sense he's losing an overall view of the thing.

I call to him in the other room where he often sits working all through the night.

'How's it going, Mort?'

'I'm looking at a lot of interfaces here. Think of them with seams. Imagine all the interfaces have seams, and none of the seams wants to fit together with the others.'

There's nothing I can do to help. There was never anything I could do, and Mort has never been a guy who seemed he needed help in any case. I remember my brother making things more difficult for himself as a kid by wanting to juggle with his *left* hand, or how he would go down the fire escape and come back up in the elevator to fetch something that was in the next room, and I wonder if he's still choosing the longest way round. Morton sits staring at imploding diagrams, and those glances over his shoulder aren't glances any more.

I wake up one night and find him whispering on my bed.

'Kiddo?'

'Yeah?'

It's funny the way when someone whispers you automatically whisper back. Here's me whispering back at Mort in order not to wake myself up.

'D'you think Pietje's going to be OK?'

'Sure she's going to—'

I clear my throat and start again in an ordinary voice.

'Sure Pietje's going to be OK. Why shouldn't she be OK?'

'You know that bar she works in?'

'Yeah.'

'I mean, have you been inside?'

'Have you?'

'It's a hostess bar. Pietje's working there as a hostess.'

'Well . . .'

I prop myself up on one elbow. I wake up.

'Is that necessarily a big deal? I mean, I work in a bar and mix drinks and flirt with single girls, and Pietje does the same with men. It depends on how you look at it.'

58

'I'm looking at it from outside. I happen to be passing by, and I see Pietje coming out of the bar with a guy and getting into a taxi.'

'Maybe the guy was just giving her a lift.'

'Then why is he paying her money?'

'What money?'

'The money he pays her before they get into the cab.'

'I don't know, Mort. But it's mostly foreigners in those places. Maybe the guy's a foreigner, and he's giving her the money and asks her to settle the fare before they get into the cab, because foreigners don't know the money and are frightened of being ripped off.'

Mort is silent for a while.

'I never thought of that. It's so simple it's brilliant.'

Mort undresses and gets into bed.

'Kiddo?'

'Yeah?'

'You know what?'

'What?'

'You won't stay bartender for long. You're much too smart.'

I've explained something to Morton. I've convinced him there's no need to be worried. Pietje's going to be OK, because the guy was a foreigner and was just giving her the fare. So simple it's brilliant. I fall back asleep, feeling happy in the cocoon of my brother's praise.

Morton decides to take up the fellowship MIT has offered him. He's been dawdling for months and suddenly he's in a real hurry to go. He'll be leaving in three weeks.

At Pietje's place we just lie in the dark and talk. Mostly it's me talking and the others listening. Mort and Pietje seem to be sort of paralysed. I tell them funny stories and all the village gossip one picks up in a bar like

Siberia. I know it's going to hit me the moment Morton's gone, but I don't feel sad in advance the way Mort and Pietje do. I wish I did. I guess I'm not a particularly mature seventeen. Not being sad in advance makes me feel emotionally inferior. Instead I act the clown and tell them all these stories, which are not too funny anyway.

I talk to my boss, who's a really nice guy. I hire Siberia for a night, and my boss charges me half price and gives me credit until Pietje and I can pay him back out of our wages. We fix Morton a terrific send-off. Everything's arranged in secret.

People in Holland are a pretty matter-of-fact, hard-headed bunch in the day-to-day routine, but they really come out of themselves on special occasions. All they need to be different from hard-headed, I mean, sometimes really *dour*, is a little excuse like someone's birthday or retirement party, and they can flick a switch into the fun mode and go completely wild. Morton has just turned twenty-one, so this is a big thing, because he's birthday and kind of retirement as well.

Morton shows up earlier than usual for a drink with the guys, and fifty or sixty people start singing 'Happy Birthday to You' the moment he comes through the door. Mort is taken completely by surprise. It's great, because the surprise matters more to the people giving it, and giving Morton a surprise is particularly satisfying. He takes off his cap like he'd just walked into a church or something and stands in the doorway and smiles. He looks round at us all with a dazed smile like he's just totally overawed. Even Dad and Helen are there, who's never got along too well with Morton. But Morton's smiling in overawed surprise and we all feel good, even Helen. It's a pretty emotional occasion.

When Mort and I get home drunk it's way past four o'clock. We slump in the living-room downstairs. I look at my brother in the chair opposite, his head thrown back, staring at the ceiling. His plane is leaving in a few hours.

'What happened to Pietje?' I ask.

'She left early. She was upset, as you can imagine.'

Mort gets up and wanders round the room. Dad's living-room is like a museum. The walls are lined with clocks, sextants and all kinds of antique mechanical gadgets displayed in glass cases. All these things belong to Dad. Helen's lived here for years, but the parakeet and the dove in two cages on the sideboard between the living-room and the kitchen are Helen's only possessions.

Helen paid two thousand guilders for the dove. Dad used to keep on mentioning how much the bird cost, but now he's grown fond of her he no longer does. My dad's a pretty tight bastard. It takes him a while to recover from spending money, even when it's not his. He leaves things in corners until he has recovered, as if he kind of resented them. This dove features a little white collar and light brown feathers. She's nice, but not more than nice. She doesn't look even remotely like she's in the two thousand guilders league. Dad had a fit, and there was a marriage crisis when Kiki moved in. But now he's used to her and Dad adores her. Kiki's now Dad's bird.

Morton stops in front of her cage.

'Bye, Kiki. Come and say goodbye.'

Kiki retreats to the end of her perch. This bird is not too strong on humans. Shy would be an understatement. When Morton slowly lifts a hand to open the cage she goes into hysterics. She flaps and squawks and cowers trembling on the floor of her cage. I can see Morton getting annoyed by the way she's responding to his attempts to be affectionate.

'Out you come.'

He grabs her and lifts her out of the cage, and Kiki

begins to shriek. It's a sound I never heard her make before, a high-pitched, long and extraordinarily piercing cry. Morton is so astonished he opens his hands. The dove flies up and flutters under the rafters, releasing a stream of brown and white feathers as she utters these piercing, anguished cries.

'What the fuck d'you think you're doing, Morton?'

Dad is standing at the door in his pyjamas.

'I don't know what happened. I don't know why – I mean, I just tried to take her out, Dad.'

'Why did you take her out?'

'I wanted to say goodbye.'

'That was a bloody stupid thing to do.'

I guess Dad says this more in shock than anger. I never heard him put Morton down like that. His face is white with rage.

'Why don't the two of you go into the kitchen or somewhere. I mean, just get out of here and let me handle this.'

We slink into the kitchen and wait out of sight behind the refrigerator while Dad is calming the bird. This takes quite a while. It's ridiculous, like we were little kids being made to stand in the corner or something. Here's his twenty-one-year-old son on stand-by to fly to MIT, hiding behind a refrigerator and maybe missing his plane because Dad first has to get a bird back into her cage.

'OK, you can come out.'

Dad has recovered but he's still pretty angry.

'I think Kiki's had a heart attack. You know, you very nearly killed that bird.'

'I'm sorry.'

Mort looks totally crushed. He goes upstairs to fetch his bags.

Dad's in the kitchen making coffee. He spoonfuls the coffee into the filter and makes cooing noises at the dove. I'm standing behind him fiddling with a wine glass. It's a habit of mine when I'm a little agitated. I pick things up and play around with them.

'*There's* a bird. There's a *nice* bird. *Coo coo coo coo coo!* He didn't mean to hurt you, course he didn't.'

'Why don't you say that to Morton instead?'

'What?'

'I guess you didn't mean to hurt Morton either, Dad, but you did. He'll be leaving the house in twenty minutes. Who's more important, Kiki or Morton? I mean, how about doing a little cooing to Morton. Before he leaves home. I think he'd appreciate it.'

'Look, I'm sorry. OK? I'll tell Morton I'm sorry.'

'Tell him you love him.'

'Of course I do. Morton knows that.'

'So telling him again would be like an extra expense, right?'

'What?'

Dad turns round and sees me fooling around with the wine glass.

'For Christ's sake be careful with that glass! That's eighteenth-century Bristol glass.'

'What if I accidentally drop it?'

'Put it down.'

'Morton took Kiki out of her cage because he wanted to say goodbye to her, and you say *that was a bloody stupid thing to do.* The thing is, Dad, you and Helen weren't around for Morton to say goodbye to, because you were in bed asleep and you only got up because Kiki woke you with that noise.'

'I'd have been up in any case.'

'No you wouldn't. You're never up before ten or eleven. You just don't care. Kiki was all there was left for Morton to say goodbye to, and you come in here and have nothing better to say than *that was a—*'

'If you drop that glass you can leave the house with Morton, and I don't want to see you back. I'm serious.'

63

'So am I. I may need some money to tide me over. Do I get a cheque or can I have it in cash?'

'You've got a fucking nerve. You won't get any money from me. Why the bloody hell should I give you money?'

'We held a party for Morton, remember? Whose idea was that? Who organised it? Has it occurred to you that someone also has to pay for it? Well, I'll trade your contribution for the Bristol glass, and I'll do what I want with it, you miserable dick, because it's mine.'

I drop the glass and it shatters on the kitchen floor.

'Go on, get out.'

I walk out of the kitchen and hear Dad shouting behind me. On my way up the stairs I pass Morton on his way down. It's like we were taking turns at this thing. It reminds me of one of those old Jack Lemmon and Walter Matthau movies.

'What's happened?' Morton asks.

'Nothing's happened. Nothing new. It's just that I hadn't noticed it until now.'

Dad doesn't clasp Morton in his arms and say he loves him. He shakes his hand and says goodbye. It's left to me to do that. I hug Morton and say I love him before he disappears at Schiphol airport, telling him that's from me *and* Dad. We could be back in Minnesota or Boston or somewhere and it's just me and Mort, passing through on our own. It's like the old patterns stick with us all our lives. Morton's already on his way through immigration when he turns back, takes off the cap with the ear-flaps and gives it to me, and then he's suddenly gone.

THIRTEEN

In some tribes a boy gets to be a man when they give him his first spear, and a girl gets to be a woman when her neck is long enough to fit three brass rings on top of each other. You're a kid yourself, and you sit watching these initiation rites on video with a one-way Heineken in your hand and they seem sort of quaint, but they're no more quaint than giving a kid a bigger bed. At some time in your life, in our tribe, you have to make this transition to a bigger bed. You stop being a kid and move into a bigger bed. When you're a kid you get into bed, close your eyes and go to sleep, wake up when the night is over and get out of bed. It's pretty straightforward. There's not an awful lot to a kid's bed. It's just a sleep box. A kid's bed isn't basically different from the place where the dog sleeps.

The adult bed opens up new dimensions. It's bigger, because you're going to need the extra space for all sorts of activities going on in the night that you didn't even dream of as a kid. The kid's bed marks a clear divide between night and day. There's no longer that divide in the adult bed. This is the loss you feel as a loss of innocence when you make the transition to the bigger bed, and days begin to run on into nights. That playground sleep like a no-man's-land between night and day, where you used to be able to hang out as a kid, is barred to you for ever.

I make the transition after I have the row with Dad and move into Pietje's place. With Morton no longer taking up space in it, Pietje's bed seems awfully big.

Naturally I talk a lot about Morton. I really miss him. When I wake up I have to get used to Morton not being there. Pietje's there, and I'm lying somewhere near the edge. It takes me a while to get used to having all that space. I feel all that space around me, which is why I keep on talking about Morton, like I'm talking him back into that space he's left in the bigger bed. Pietje doesn't really know about Morton. I feel an urge to *explain* him to her. I unpack the heavenly rucksack and make a start on the early years, Cape Cod, whale watching, all that stuff. It takes a couple of weeks of non-stop talking in bed at night to get Morton to age ten, and gradually I begin to feel better.

I have to go back home to pick up my stuff. The problem is how. I made such a terrific exit, I don't know how to follow it up. I feel like I guess an actor would feel who's left a terrific impression on the audience but has to come back on stage and spoil it, because he's forgotten to say his last line. So I wait at the corner until I see Dad and Helen going out, and then I sneak in and fetch my stuff. This isn't my style. I come out feeling like trash.

Pietje and I make love. We do this a lot in the bigger bed. We fuck like rabbits. She curls up on her side and I fuck her from behind, she spreads her legs and sprawls over me and fucks me sitting on top. We're pretty experimental. We have a lot of fun. But it's odd, there are these moments when I feel self-conscious. Pietje has jaunty tits and an arse with a lot of swagger, the whole shoot, as Dad would say, she's a real *woman*, and sometimes I find it difficult to believe it's me who's handling all of this. I'm into this adult stuff, and I'm em*barr*assed.

There never used to be anything embarrassing when Morton was around. I mean, we laughed a lot, and it was like more of a game. Now I'm alone with Pietje we're getting down to serious sex. It's just me and Pietje fucking like hell in that bed, and the whole thing is getting tremendously personal.

I get so involved telling the story of Morton's life that I fail to hear Pietje's silence. In the meantime Morton's eleven. We're approaching the Great Divide, the five lost years, wiped clean out of my brother's biography because unfortunately I wasn't around. We have to skip that part, and pretty soon Pietje should be coming into the story. But she doesn't. Here's where Pietje draws the line. She tells me I've got to stop talking about my brother and start being myself. This is kind of an ultimatum.

'Either Morton or me.'

She takes me out to Steenhoven to meet her folks, and it's like her dad with his MS gets substituted for me with my Morton. This is the bone that Pietje gnaws, or the bone that gnaws Pietje. As the corner house off Singel goes into decline and the house overlooking the dunes in Steenhoven is ascendant, Pietje drops out of my family and I drop into hers. We take out our washing for her mother to do. We sit in the living-room drinking coffee and eating her mother's home-made cake. I'm seventeen and a half and on my way to a junior partnership in the Steenhoven house. It feels like I'm already married. Pietje's hand is always out on the table dabbing for crumbs in her parents' house, and they're still sticking to her fingers when we arrive back in Amsterdam.

'Dad doesn't approve of what I'm doing.'

'But you've told him you're working in a restaurant.'

'That's what I told him, but it's not what he believes.'

'Do you have to have your dad's approval?'

67

She turns this back on me in a flash, as if it's what she's been waiting to say to me all along.

'Do you have to have Morton's?'

'I guess the difference is I never had to grovel to get Mort's approval the way you do with your dad. He gave it of his own free will and didn't expect anything back.'

'That's where you're wrong.'

'Oh? Well, now that you bring the matter up, are we allowed to talk about Morton again?'

'No. What's my dad expecting back?'

'I don't know. If I were your dad I'd want to fuck you. You'll only ever get your dad's approval the day you get into bed with him. These family ties are as incestuous as hell.'

Pietje colours, her lips slightly parted. She looks really sexy. Pietje is aroused.

It's a Saturday night, and I'm working late at Siberia. Pietje shows up with a couple of girls at two o'clock in the morning.

'Oy! Bartender!'

I come over in this shirt with a Russian collar. The Russian look is in and a lot of guys who wear these shirts look like serfs, but I guess I carry it off. I get a lot of tips, especially from girls. I do my bartender act.

'Ladies?'

Lights kind of bounce off these three high-breasted broads sitting at the counter. They're all gorgeous. The red-headed Australian girl called Trixy looks like she was poured out with a bottle of wine. You don't get that kind of warm complexion much in Amsterdam. You get more these North Sea coast types like Anita, cooler girls with wide-open faces in which there are no secrets. Pietje is darker, tousled, secrets one can only guess at in an Indonesian cast to her eyelids that comes out late at night.

The girls have had a few drinks. They park their tits on the counter, roll their eyes and order three vodkas.

'Like your shirt, baby. It's cute.'

'Honey, I changed my mind. Gimme a Singapore sling.'

I take the vodka back and fix Trixy a Singapore sling. The girls have been to see a movie. They're fooling around doing this Lauren Bacall stuff. It has them in hysterics.

I bring the Singapore sling. Trixy and Pietje continue speaking English. Anita switches to Dutch.

'Don't you remember me?'

'Not off hand. Give me a clue.'

'Humidity.'

'What?'

'You kissed me at a dance.'

It's embarrassing. I mean, how's it possible to have forgotten kissing this Anita?

'You didn't know how to say 'humidity' in Dutch, and I told you.'

'Jesus. Anita Vermaat. In the *buurthuis* four years ago. Yeah, it was really hot at that dance. Where've you been all this time?'

'In South Africa.'

'Humididity,' Trixy interrupts in English. Her speech is getting pretty slurred. 'I got *that* much. What are you guys talking about?'

A group of German tourists is waiting at the far end of the counter and I have to fix them some beers. I notice Anita crossing the room to the phone booth in the corner. Trixy and Pietje go into a huddle. The Germans eye them over while I'm pulling the beers, and then they eye me in my Russian shirt, and their verdict is clearly: guy's a serf. Bartenders have to live with this. We come in for a lot of resentment from single males on account of our privileged access to single girls. Hell, it's our job.

Coming back to Anita. You wouldn't recognise her. I check her figure out as she's standing with one arm leaning against the wall, talking on the phone. She's grown up a *lot* in four years.

I head back to the girls at the other end of the counter, straight into trouble.

'Didn't you have a brother?' goes Trixy.

'I still do.'

'He had an unusual name.'

The girls have set this thing up. Pietje comes in on cue.

'Morton. Want to hear the rhyme about Morton?'

'Oh, *yeah*.'

Trixy again, feeding Pietje her lines.

'There was a crooked guy, he had a crooked dick, he laid about the little girls with his big fat stick.'

I wipe the counter in front of the girls.

'That's only medium funny, Pietje. I've heard funnier rhymes.'

'Who said it was meant to be a funny rhyme? You know what the trouble is with this guy? The trouble is his brother. Mention Morton and his sense of humour drops down dead.'

'Why don't you shut up.'

'He can't take criticism of his brother. Brother Morton is a fucking icon. But deep down Kiddo's envious. They put on this brotherly act, and deep down they hate each other's guts.'

My hand just flies out and whaps Pietje. I can't believe it. I never hit anyone in my life.

Pietje's eyes are wide open.

'See? That's how much the truth hurts.'

I go to the back of the bar and start washing glasses, feeling just terrible. Suddenly I hate what I'm doing. I hate my life. I hate Pietje. Most of all I hate myself. I find an excuse to go out to the storeroom, and when I come back Trixy and Pietje have gone. The German tourists have gone too. It's four o'clock in the morning and Jan is closing down. There are just a few couples left at the tables, and this Anita, who's finally got herself off the phone, sitting at the counter drinking vodka pretty much on her own.

'Hey, where'd everybody go all of a sudden?'

'We just had an argument. I'd rather not talk about it. Let's talk about something else. Does your dad by any chance have something to do with the fruit industry in South Africa?'

'Yeah, matter of fact he does. How the hell did you know that?'

'OK, right now I'm a bartender, but there's this guy from the careers office who happened to mention an opportunity in the fruit industry in South Africa a couple of months back . . .'

This Anita knows all about the fruit industry in South Africa, I mean, she really knows the country, she's lived there, and her dad is an important guy in the fruit business. Anita is critical of some of the things that go on over there, like the way white people put down black, but pretty soon we're on to surfing and sunsets and we get all that apartheid stuff behind us, and I can see the chips piling up on the credit side of South Africa really fast. I see the mirage of a future taking shape. There are things that have to be sorted out with Pietje, and apartheid, that also has to be sorted out, definitely, but not too far beyond I can see an open country where people feel kind of clean and cool. Jan has thrown the last customer out and is boozing in a corner with his pals, while I'm hitting the vodka with Anita and getting high as I watch these new horizons rolling back around the counter.

Maybe this is why it happens with Anita, because when I go out to the yard to leave the leftovers for the cats and lock up at the back I don't have anything particular in mind, but maybe Anita does, I guess she's in the mood, and this thing just happens. I come into the passage where it's as dark as hell and I don't even see Anita until I walk right into her. I mean, this Anita knows why she's standing there in the dark. She knows exactly what she has in mind. I hear her humming as she kisses me, and I've never been kissed by a girl who was humming at the same time, and it's nice, the way Anita hums and kisses at the same time. Then she asks me where we can go, and I say what do you mean go at this time of the night, go where, we're the last bar to close in town, and she says go *here*, putting her hand on my dick, and without even thinking about it I say well, Anita, how about the storeroom you're standing right in front of. Anita thinks the storeroom is a swell idea.

There's always a whole lot of junk floating around my mind. At school this was a major hazard, with me always moving over disintegrating pack ice and drifting away on some island while the rest of the class stayed put on solid ground. Storeroom gives maybe a wrong idea of the amenities at Siberia, certainly for this kind of thing, where I'm perched with my butt on three cases of Heineken and running my hands up Anita's thighs, but not in a storeroom at all, more a crazily lit cupboard with the light bulb drooping on a strip of knotted flex just above my head, wondering about all sorts of stuff other than what's happening right here and now. Anita has pulled up her T-shirt, like she's having to remind me my hands might start moving some place else, and they do, as though I'm not having any say in the matter. It comes as a bit of a shock to find myself comparing Anita's breasts with Pietje's, because it's Pietje I have at the back of my mind and then I realise what I'm doing, and for a moment I think *what are you doing with this Anita here*, until Pietje's breasts fade out of the insert and it's just Anita's up there on the screen. She's asking me to do, like, *math* with her, she says, you know, ask me sums of multiplication and division, like three times ninety-four and fifty-six divided by seven, and no girl ever asked me to do *that* while I was squeezing her breasts. This Anita has a pretty unusual streak that comes out when she takes off her clothes, because she really likes the way I take snips at her nipples with my fingers as I ask her nine times nine, she's just ace at math, go on, she says, make them harder, and we're getting into really big numbers when I put my hands under her arse and lift her astride me and the Heinekens beneath us start to creak. Her arms are clasped behind my neck, her tits pressed against my face, and Anita says she likes the way I *grab* her, she says bite me so it hurts a tiny bit, and I do, and between bites I'm mumbling three hundred and sixty-seven divided by forty-two, and she doesn't know the answer, instead she squeezes me with her thighs and moans and we surf all the way into the sunset on the creaking cases of Heineken.

It's daylight when I get into bed beside Pietje. I'm back from the first outing with my spear and the result has been disaster. Pietje has a bruise coming up on one side of her face, another she doesn't yet know about will soon be on its way. I can't flick the switch like I used to, just falling asleep and waking up when the night is over. For a long time I lie awake. I look at Pietje's sleeping face and say I'm sorry to her in her sleep. It's the same remorse-tenderness crap I could see through as a kid when I was woken up by my dad and heard him pleading outside Moo's bedroom door in the middle of the night. I'm an adult all right. I've graduated to the bigger bed, and there's no longer that easy divide between night and day there used to be when I was a kid.

73

FOURTEEN

A grain of sand has slipped in somewhere. The action's not as smooth as it was. Pietje's mood has changed. She's distant, and I don't know why.

It's not the thing with Anita. Naturally I tell her about Anita right away, and Pietje's pretty upset. But Pietje isn't jealous of Anita. It's a one-off with Anita, and I don't see her again.

In some way I can't quite figure out, Pietje is jealous of Morton.

I've stopped talking about Morton, with the result that I've started thinking about *not* talking about Morton. The silence is eerie. I wait for Pietje to bring the subject up. Morton has gone, and Pietje was very fond of him, and after that unpleasant scene in Siberia months have passed without her ever mentioning his name.

Out of the blue it comes to me that there's something between Pietje and Morton that I don't know about. I ask her. She denies it. My instincts tell me Pietje's lying.

For a long time I live with this feeling of her lying. It gets under my skin, I can't get rid of it. It gets into my system, and gradually the feeling Pietje is lying to me begins to fabricate the things she's lying to me about.

Pietje's not talking about Morton is like she's covering

something up. I nag her, in a jokey sort of way, and then in a not so jokey way. The hole where my brother used to be is a vacuum in which I can feel Pietje's lie growing. Is she in love with Morton and not with me? Was he better in bed with his bigger dick? What's she been up to behind my back?

I wake Pietje up in the middle of the night to ask her these questions. I drive us both crazy.

Then I remember the guy Morton saw getting into a taxi with Pietje. I start hanging around outside the place where Pietje works. I spy on her. But what I'm seeing in my mind doesn't happen on the street. I'm seeing Pietje coming out of the bar in the action replay, as Morton described it, and taking money from a guy before getting into a cab with him. In the action replay this keeps on happening. You've seen it, and after you've seen it a dozen times the action replay looks a lot more convincing than something that's not happening. There's a crazy logic in this kind of thing.

I have to confront Pietje. I have to have it out with her.

'Morton says he saw you coming out of the bar. He says he saw a guy give you money, and then you got into a taxi with the guy. Was he giving you money to sleep with him?'

'It's not true.'

'OK, so why would Morton make up a stupid story like that?'

'Ask Morton.'

One of them has to be lying. Both alternatives are equally bad and I can't face up to either of them. Morton called once when he got to America, but he didn't leave a number for me to call him back. I don't call Morton because I don't know where to reach him and Pietje's unreachable even when we're lying in the same bed. I pretend to myself there's some other explanation. I turn myself into the lie.

This is not such a great time for me. I get disillusioned. The way this thing cracks up with Pietje is slow and painful. I feel us kind of drying out, losing some sort of moisture that used to hold us together. We come apart, the sole cracks and dries right off the shoe, and one day there's no longer a shoe any more but just two pieces lying around, with a grain of sand between.

After breaking up with Pietje everything else starts breaking up, too. I get arrested on a couple of drugs charges, and the third time this happens the welfare people have me taken into psychiatric care to keep me out of trouble. I spend time in various clinics talking to a lot of guys. All these guys are basically telling me the same stuff that Pietje's been telling me, which is that I have a major problem with my elder brother, and that I have to get shot of him in order to shake it off.

In a way, I guess I do. I become independent after a fashion. I move into the place off Prinsengracht where I'm living now, still on the list of condemned buildings four years on. I don't go back to my job at Siberia. Instead I get a job modelling for advertising agencies. I kick the drug habit and keep myself in trim. I have to look after my body.

I'm back on the level.

I see Pietje now and again, but apart from a couple of postcards, with no address, I hear nothing from Morton for almost a year. And then this letter arrives, just out of the blue.

FIFTEEN

Dear Kiddo,

Did you get the postcards I sent en route?

If you checked the post marks you'll have noticed that they were mailed from all over America. Probably you didn't check, and you won't have noticed anything. The cards come from all over America because I bought a car as soon as I arrived in the country and I've been on the road ever since. When I reached the turning to MIT I kept on driving. I never went to MIT.

This wasn't a premeditated thing, but it wasn't something done on impulse, either. Behind what may seem to be just a whim there was a recognition of something instantly familiar the moment I touched down in Boston. It's like the spirit had always stayed put here, Kiddo, and the wanderings of my body elsewhere in the years between have been the incarnations of an estranged spirit. Somewhere the spirit has a place where it belongs. People can intuit this place, and they go out and look for it, and a few of them arrive. Despite the thousands of miles I've driven, the months I've been on the road, this journey has really been a quest in search of something that is not moving, the return to a centre of original stillness which is the sense of my belonging.

Moo has to do with this, because of the strangeness between Moo and me, but it goes beyond her. You were her chosen, which is why you had to be mine. But things went the way they did, and in the end it was no longer Moo who mattered, it was you. I knew you were her chosen the moment you were born. I learned to kiss you and stroke you when you were lying in her lap, and in my heart I wanted to kill you.

I have cancer and I'm dying, and the doctors have given me not more than twelve or eighteen months to live. There are things we have to talk about, Kiddo.

I ran Moo to ground near San Jose, where she's living in a trailer with a guy not much older than I am. Her energy's unchanged. You still walk into a buzz of warm vulgarity and chatter and the cloud of cheap perfume surrounding her. It was the most relaxed time we ever spent together, because it was the first time we were meeting honestly as the strangers we've always been.

She asked about you and Dad, but we didn't talk much about the past. The cat had just given birth to five kittens and we talked with them in the middle while I fixed a video recorder she wanted to throw out. Mostly we talked about her video recorder and her cats. Don't think there was anything strained about this. It wasn't as if we wanted to avoid touching on the past. The past didn't exist.

The past had no existence in Moo's trailer, and it didn't exist anywhere else either. I stopped looking for it. I didn't think about it. I had other things to think about.

On those twelve-lane highways, when you just keep moving, the verges quickly begin to blur. The highways have speed limits, but the people travelling down them don't. Does that make sense to you? Our speed is relative to things like the size of our brain and the mass of data it processes. The greater the mass, the more we have to accelerate.

We're information consumers all the time, consuming massively, at massive speed. The impressions are drops of water evaporating instantly on a white-hot surface. There is no retention, only the processing and disposal of an ever denser mass of signals with ever shorter life cycles. Human speed is an equation involving mass per units of time per units of processing power. It's simple. Past has to be jettisoned to accommodate present. Here's a human machine on the road whose disintegration is the logical outcome of how it was built.

Driving without stopping for months on end, you rack up a terrific input of country hurried through. It gets addictive, Kiddo. It's Saturday night out in Amsterdam. First you don't want to stop, then you can't. In the end you get just a blur which is kind of intoxicating. The more you see, the quicker it's over and the less it matters. You're in constant motion. You're not in place any more.

All these people rushing down the highways are dying in their cars, but they don't know it, because unlike me none of them believe in death. Except me. I'm the lucky guy, Kiddo. I have the privilege of riding in the car of triumph, like one of those victorious Roman generals, with a slave crouching at his feet and reminding his master that he's not immortal, because to believe so is hubris, which the gods will punish. No one can hear what this prompter is saying who is travelling in my car. When I listen to it in the rush of wind on the highway as I leave the San Francisco clinic where they diagnose my cancer and tell me that I'm dying, all my senses sharpen in the narrowing focus on this one bright ring, and when I hear it whispering through the inflight console as I fly over the Pacific I look down at the glittering sea with a feeling of exhilaration.

When you were born, and I saw how Moo took to you, I became so jealous I wanted to kill you. I used to pinch you behind her back. Once I had a pillow in my hands with the idea of smothering you. Wanting to kill you is the first memory I have of you. Wanting to kill you was my first emotional attachment to you. Instead, I coddled you. For Moo's benefit I put on a show of loving my younger brother to earn my mother's approval and make me seem less of a stranger to her. I told myself I loved you. I loved you by an act of will, which in time became second nature to me, until I'd forgotten how my closest bond with you began.

I got home from Leiden one evening after I'd received my doctorate there, and picked up the mail in the hall and came up to the attic where you told me you'd quit school. You were feeling very bitter. You called me *the golden boy*. Remember?

The differences between us had become too obvious to ignore. Me with my doctorate. You a dropout, starting life empty-handed at sixteen and feeling that Dad didn't give a shit about you. The envy and bitterness had never come out of you like that before. It gave me a terrible shock. I saw just how effectively I'd carried out a plan I thought I'd long forgotten. I saw how I'd been holding you so close to me that I'd smothered you.

Then Pietje came along. Here was another woman we were competing for. We may have pretended we weren't, but we were. I went to Pietje behind your back and asked her to leave Amsterdam, and come with me to America. I tried to oust you, but I failed. Pietje refused. Did she mention this to you? I guess she'll have told you about it herself. I feel really bad about it, Kiddo. On its own, this thing with Pietje is a betrayal and unforgivable, only it doesn't stand on its own. It's more complicated. It's more like the consummation of a betrayal that has been hanging over since you were born, and I'm not sure if Pietje can be expected to understand that. You have to see the self-betrayal before it became a betrayal of you. You have to understand there's a differ-ence between how a thing began and what it became, which was a love for you, *despite everything*, Kiddo, and which remained in place even when I was attempting to take Pietje away from you.

I want you to look inside me and rid yourself of any illusions. The illusion you must get rid of is that any feeling can be pure, *any* feeling, which is something I had to learn from you that night; except that you still have this one blind spot around your elder brother, and the purity you've always taken for granted in his feelings for you. Living up to your expectations was more of a burden for me than you ever realised.

Why is my body sick of me? And why with this dis-ease? Sometimes I think I've spent my life too much inside the kind of mono-culture that flourishes around over-specialisation, and I can see my cancer as the logi-cal outcome of a one-sided kind of health.

What is cancer? Cancer is the disease of hypertrophy and acceleration. Cancer cells proliferate uncontrollably and form metastases, a triumphant achievement from their point of view, but at the cost of overrunning the organism as a whole.

Remember those drawings that used to hang up in the loft? You know, when I try to visualise this disease, what comes to my mind are an engineer's construction draw-ings, exploding an object into its parts. It's a nightmare of a drawing gone wrong. The parts keep on exploding and generating new strings of parts, until they are no longer parts of anything, because they overrun the whole, and obliterate it.

Hypertrophy and overspecialisation may be the char-acteristics of a species approaching extinction. What my senses tell me is less and less relevant to what I'm being told by my brain. The brain's orders of magnitude are far beyond anything I can sensually appreciate or measure.

Sometimes I feel I've gone blind. I feel there's no longer a right proportion between my senses and my brain. It's as if they belonged to different evolutionary orders.

Perhaps my body is missing a sense of balance. Perhaps the proliferation of the cancer cells takes place as compensation for the sense of wholeness that is missing in me. I always envied you that, what I felt was your instinctive grasp of things. My view of wholeness has become a perception of the exploding parts. The view of the organism has been obliterated by the proliferation of its cancerous cells.

If you can catch cancer the way you catch cold, I can nail it down to the day, because here's the image of it that has surfaced in my consciousness since you called me *the golden boy*, an image of the lifelong rancour that hadn't gone away, as I thought it had, but formed metastases and proliferated in hiding inside my body. I've been holding you so close to me that in the end I have smothered myself.

This isn't just a confession, Kiddo. It's kind of like a testament as well. This is why I'm wandering round the world. I always wanted to go to China. Do you remember that weird book about burial places? I guess you won't. Some years back I read about these villages with their burial places in north China, and I spent a long time travelling until I found one. The place was called Three Hills. I lived in a hut on the edge of a village called Three Hills where I could look out the window and count them, three dunes rising out of a wilderness.

There was a time when the village was called Beside the Lake. But China is a miraculous country where lakes begin to move when the wind blows and the dunes shift, and after half a century the lake had settled down some place else. The dunes stayed put when the wind had taken away the lake, so the village called itself

Three Hills instead. The people dug trenches and diverted streams and started a fish farm to make up for the livelihood that had gone away with the lake.

About as many people live in Three Hills as used to live in Beside the Lake. That's a hundred and forty-seven inhabitants, more or less what the population has been for as long as anyone can remember. You might think things would have changed when the lake went away, but things didn't, because the folks brought in the fish farm instead. Big deal, I hear you saying. Well, why I'm telling you about Three Hills is not on account of the wandering lake stuff but the graveyard out back. The bus stops on the main road and you walk down a track to the village. Village, that's a total of about fifty dwellings. You might call it a suburb of the graveyard, because when you're through the village and into the graveyard you arrive at a city.

There are thousands of people lying buried in the plain behind Three Hills. It's a city of the dead, made of gravestones, incomparably bigger than the village from which the dead came. The inhabitants of Beside the Lake and Three Hills have been carrying their dead out to the plain behind the village for many hundreds of years. The ancestors have kept on piling up their stones out there, and when you look at the plot next door where their hundred and forty-seven living descendants huddle there's no mistaking that the world of the living is the shanty town, and any perspectives of the power and the glory are in those stone monuments to the vast army of the dead accumulating in the plain.

In China's old world the living arranged their lives in accordance with what they saw as the needs of the dead. The landscape of ancient China's civilisation took shape with this in mind. The sites of towns and dwellings, of roads and bridges, were determined with reference to the haunts of the dead. The dead were the immeasurably

83

greater majority. The living listened respectfully to the dead in the arrangement of their lives.

People must have been aware in a way we no longer are that life is an exception to the universal rule of death. They perceived themselves on a narrow strip of light surrounded by an infinite darkness. They were the inheritors of the living who were now dead, and they listened to the dead, and contemplated their own future in the darkness not out of fear and ignorance but wonder. They were fully aware of the fragility of their narrow strip of light. They were fully aware of the finiteness of the present which they had inherited from their ancestors, and which their descendants in turn would inherit from them.

Three Hills and its burial ground reflect the preoccupation of life with death for as long as there have been thinking people around on this planet. That's how we and they stack up — the living in their passing briefness, the dead in an enduring immensity of nothingness. The dead have the majority vote. They stick around. They supervise their cults. There are always more and more of them. The dead matter to the living.

Except the dead no longer have the majority vote. The living are now the majority. By the end of the second millennium more people will be alive on earth than ever lived before. *There'll be more people living at the end of the twentieth century than the sum total of all the people who have died in the history of the human race.*

Just sit there and think about that for five minutes. For me this is a pathological number, a statistic even more frightening than the dream into which it flows, my recurrent nightmare of the drawing of exploding parts overrunning and obliterating the whole. The voice of the dead is a minority voice that has fallen silent. We can't hear the dead any more, Kiddo. We live in an illusion of life without death.

This is my testament, Kiddo. When I come back to

Holland I want to go with you to see Rembrandt's painting of the anatomy lesson of Dr Tulp in Den Haag, and I shall make provisions in my will for my body to be left to medical science.

In the Renaissance an anatomy lesson was a public occasion, taking place at one of the great anatomical theatres in Amsterdam or Leiden. They're called theatres because they were places of entertainment. There's a description of them in a Dutch book I came across in a shop in San Francisco, which I still have with me. It's in old Dutch, so it may be easier for you if I write it in English, but just listen to it in Dutch for a moment, and read on, and see if you can hear what I can hear beneath the sound of the gongs.

'*Omme den begeerigen Leser ten vollen te moghen te vreden stellen soo sal ick de Beschrijvinghe van dese plaetse wat naerder ondersoecken ende beschrijven* . . . in order to acquaint the curious reader with all this in a proper manner, I shall give a close account and description of the particulars of this place, and I shall begin with its arrangement. Apart from the circular place in the middle, where the anatomising is done, the *theatrum* is divided into six circles or galleries which rise obliquely, enabling one to see with ease and unhampered what dissecting is being done below. In the circle that lies at the bottom, there has been placed a rotating table on which *the body destined to be anatomised* is to be placed. This is covered with a white linen sheet and draped with a black cloth. At this table only the professor who performs the dissection has his place, the *anathomicus* of the academy, whom I shall here mention to his honour inasmuch as at this place he has anatomised several bodies of men, women, *and sundry beasts,* to the unspeakably great profit and advancement of those that have attended, understood, and *perceived this properly*. In the first circle, immediately around the anatomical table, the professors are seated and certain other persons of rank and dignity; in the two following circles, which are provided with separate boxes, there stand the surgeons and all the students of medicine; in the subsequent circles all the other students as well as whoever else has *the desire and inclination* to follow and observe the performance. All around these ranks there are separately placed in careful arrangement seven frames, that is skeletons, of persons male and female who have been put together with utmost skill by means of copper wires. Some of these hold sundry banners in their hands whereto have been affixed various devices and mottoes in the Latin tongue bearing upon the *brittleness* and *fleeting quality* of Man's body . . .'

I can hear cigarette ash scattering in an ashtray under the whir of a fly's wings.

Take care of yourself, Kiddo. I can't tell you how much I've missed you. I'll be seeing you soon, at the latest by Christmas, and until then as ever

With all my love –

Morton

SIXTEEN

I'm in Indonesia making a Tango fruit juice commercial when this letter arrives. After the crack-up with Pietje I'm into an incredibly lucrative phase of modelling teen fashions and soft drinks. Forget about North Sea fisheries and warehouse management. Forget all that crap. At last I've had a break. We do the commercials in scenic locations all over the world, and these days I'm travelling first class. I'm screwing entire advertising casts of girls and making money and having a hell of a time. My life is totally superficial. I just don't want to know about anything else. It's a very relaxing life. After Pietje I don't want to get personally involved with a woman again. I've no idea where Pietje even is, and I don't particularly care. I've not heard from Pietje for over six months.

On Christmas Eve I get back from Indonesia and I go straight round to the house with all this junk I've bought as presents for Helen and Dad. You buy ethnic jewellery made of shells and weird stuff like strips of plant fibre for washing your hair, which seems hilarious on site, but when you take it out of your suitcase and put it under a Christmas tree inside a Dutch house it looks like junk.

There's no one at home. I guess they're all out partying some place. I hang around, waiting for the guys to

87

come back. I'm jet-lagged. I go upstairs to take a shower, but I'm so tired I fall asleep instead. It's only after I wake up and come back downstairs that I notice the letter stuck in the mirror in the hall. Recognising my brother's handwriting, I feel my heart give sort of a jump.

I'm still in the middle of reading Morton's letter when Helen and Dad walk into the house. Dad's grim, Helen's crying, I'm still reeling. This definitely isn't the best of homecomings.

Dad says Morton arrived at Schiphol ten days ago and went straight into hospital. I can't believe it. He's in the intensive unit in a critical condition. Morton's dying. At the outside he only has a couple of months to live. I've just been reading this in Morton's letter, and I can't believe it, but already it's come true. Dad and Helen talk in a sniffy, and-where-have-*you*-been tone of voice, like they're showing me they think my attitude is frivolous, and they're putting me down.

How hypocritical can you get?

Death provides the onlookers with an easy emotional ride, and Helen and Dad who were pretty casual about Morton during his life are falling all over him the moment he starts dying.

Morton stays in intensive care and at first I'm not allowed to see him. When I do, I get a hell of a shock. My brother looks like a ghost. He has tubes coming out of his prick and his arse. It hurts me just to look at him. I sit there for a couple of hours, watching him in his sleep while stuff is oozing out of the tubes, feeling terrifically uncomfortable as I listen to those Christmas carols out in the corridor. I've brought him the Indonesian plant fibre shampoo, because it's the kind of weird thing that Morton enjoys, but he doesn't wake up for me to give it to him, and when I leave the hospital I'm so miserable I throw it in the trash can at the exit.

While Mort's out of action I keep on reading his letter. This stuff about Morton wanting to kill me being how he got emotionally attached to me is just bizarre. I don't know what to do with it. It doesn't get through to me. I picture him cruising down all those highways and hanging out in the village in China, travelling right around the world and having conversations with all these dead guys, which is pretty odd when you consider that on his travels round the world Mort doesn't mention a single conversation he had with any living person except his mother.

Mort's always been a loner, but this is different. There's an awful sense of loneliness hanging around his letter. Maybe the loneliness has something to do with the fact that he's dying, but I'm seeing this the other way round, and my guess is that Morton's dying has something to do with his loneliness. It makes me feel pretty bad, because as his brother I should have done more to keep him company. But the fact is I'm still so shocked by the sight of Morton lying in hospital with tubes coming out of him that I don't really think too much about his letter. It's like it was already out of date and I'm waiting to get on to the next instalment, so for the time being I put the letter away. It'll be a long time before I look at it again.

Reviewing the reels in the heavenly rucksack, I see Morton and me fooling around and having fun as kids, but whenever I can stop a frame and move in on Morton's face I always see a look of complete seriousness. It's not like I'm imagining this. The kiddy photos of my brother and me all show the same thing. The dead-pan look was kind of his trademark. Mort was the Buster Keaton kid. I used to be able to hear him chuckling underneath, as if he was listening to something inside himself, but that's not what I hear now.

Now I can hear the whispers Morton heard, and I

know he was listening to them with dread. There's a trail of clues all the way through that letter he wrote me, and I guess I'd have picked them up if I'd been looking for clues, but I wasn't at the time. Pietje says I'm very naive, and maybe I am, but that's a part of how you are when you love someone very much.

Mort comes out of hospital literally drained. There's nothing more they can do for him there.

The terminal cancer puts the spotlight on Mort again. It gets him the star billing. Helen says all the people in the Singel neighbourhood are being so considerate. That's certainly the way it looks. They arrive laden with fruit and flowers and stuff, but underneath I can sense their relief, even a kind of secret glee, that it's someone else who's got this awful thing. Dad and Helen speak in lowered voices, sneaking around the house on tiptoe while Mort lies in the attic room upstairs.

He feels the emptiness, I guess, which is why he wants a lot of people around him when the hospital sends him home. I move back into the house to keep him company. I cultivate a breezy, maybe over-breezy manner, partly as a reaction to all that considerateness oozing through the house, partly because I'm devastated and just don't know how to handle my dying brother. All I can do is to keep him company for the rest of the way.

The attic becomes almost like a coffee house again, just as it used to be when we were kids at school. People are drifting in and out all the time, Harko and Billy and welfare brats like Kip who'd OD'd not long after Morton died. Dad and Helen think Morton needs a kind of nursing-room thing with flowers and white sheets, but Morton says it's not a funeral parlour he wants, he wants a coffee house. So the kids are allowed to stay in the attic and make their racket and stink and Helen has to take her stuff back downstairs.

90

One day Pietje shows up. She simply wanders in one afternoon, like she'd just been round the block to buy cigarettes.

When I'm with her on her own I ask her if what Morton said about wanting her to go with him to America is true, and she says it is. Pietje's pretty offhanded about this, like it's not a big deal. She doesn't want to talk about it, and she tells me just to drop it. Later I know Morton was waiting for Pietje to come back before he could wind things up the way he wanted. Morton was sorry about what he'd done. He just hung in until Pietje showed up and he could tell her so.

It's a few days after Pietje shows up that we carry Morton downstairs and put him in the minibus and drive to Den Haag to see Rembrandt's picture of the anatomy lesson. Maybe the corpse has made something of an impression on the kids, but not much else. Den Haag is a really boring place. When we get back from the outing, all the kids gather upstairs and Morton tells them about the arrangements he's made with Amsterdam University.

He's bequeathing his body to the medical faculty on the condition that anyone who wants to can attend the autopsy. He tells the kids that if anyone wants to they're welcome to come along. If they think this is maybe a rather weird kind of invitation, so are a lot of the other parties they've been along to in their lives, and they don't let on that this is particularly different. They just nod and roll their joints, and turn up the music.

Dad and Helen can't understand why Morton chooses to surround himself with the likes of Kip and Harko, whom they regard as the neighbourhood trash. Dad and Helen would like Morton to *go out in style*, but they lie about this all the time, feeding him this crap about how he's going to get well and secretly plotting how they can get Morton to *go out in style*, not for his benefit but their own, because they're worried it doesn't look too good the way Mort is doing his dying, and maybe the neighbours will get a wrong impression.

But Mort doesn't like these embalming procedures they're getting started on before he's dead. He prefers the coffee-house atmosphere up in the attic where he's surrounded by kids who've spent quite a lot of their short lives looking over the brink, and who are completely unsentimental about what they see on the other side. Nothing's on the other side. Dying is the mega-trip, the terminal black-out. They don't give Morton crap about getting well, because they know he won't. They don't have this older-generation idea that anyone's ever *been* well.

Morton's in a lot of pain towards the end, despite all the pain-killers the doctors give him. My brother's way of going out in style is not to let on that he's in pain, but when I hear him groaning in the night I put on the light and go and talk to him, to take his mind off the pain. He tells me he's made a mess of his life, and at least he wants to get his death right.

In secret he's made his own arrangements.

One night we talk about his will. This is a pact. We get into the solemn stuff I've always been a sucker for, and Morton reinforces this by referring to his will as a *pact*. By the terms of my pact with Morton, I have been appointed my brother's *executor* and *sole heir*. He's totally matter-of-fact when he says he's leaving me not only his books and his patents, which some day may be quite valuable, but the inner organs of his body, conserved in methyl alcohol as part of the deal he's made with the medical faculty of the university.

I ask Mort why he wants to leave me his inner organs. Mort says he doesn't want to just vanish. He's worried by the thought of vanishing right away and all in one go. He'd like to stick around for a while after he's dead. I tell

Mort not to worry about that. He'll be sticking around in any case, without his inner organs in jars to remind me. I mean, there's absolutely no way I'm ever going to forget my brother.

This still doesn't satisfy Mort. He gets pretty agitated, because he has difficulty breathing and talking at the same time. He asks if I'm saying I don't want them. Frankly, I'm not too keen on the whole autopsy idea, and I have to do a little lying in this area, which Morton would once have homed in on right away. Left to my own devices, I'd have been a natural liar, but with Morton around I grew up *having* to be honest. Whereas now, when I say sure, of course I want the jars, he doesn't pick up the lie. He says it makes dying a lot easier for him to imagine me having him around, and perhaps it'll also make things easier for me when he's gone. He says it's not like he has to be on display or anything. He'd be happy to settle for his jars to go into a cupboard. From the way he's rambling on I can tell that Mort's mind is beginning to wander in strange places, and so I say it's a deal, let's do it that way, and Mort makes me promise, and I give him my promise, because I'm his *sole heir*, and we don't talk about his inner organs again.

Morton's made his own arrangements. The coffee house is in session as usual when this guy walks in one afternoon. He's a big blond guy of about thirty. I never saw him before. He says he's a friend of Morton's and would like to see him.

I take him into the next room where Morton is lying in bed and Pietje is sitting on a chair by the window with Erasmus on her knee. Morton is no longer conscious all the time, but he looks up and sees this guy and I can tell that he's there and recognises him at once. His eyes open really wide and he tries to sit up. The guy lays the palm of his hand on Morton's chest and lets it rest there. Morton and this blond guy look at each other but don't say anything. My brother closes his eyes again after a while, and the blond guy gets up and shuts the door.

Pietje and I watch him take stuff out of his coat pockets and lay it on the table. There's a flask, a coil of tube, and a needle. He attaches the tube to the flask and puts the flask on the shelf above the bed. He sits down by the bed and takes Morton's arm and sort of strokes it.

'OK?'

Morton has his eyes closed. He just nods.

The blond guy looks for a vein and inserts the needle. Then he gets to his feet, turns the flask upside down and hangs it over the tip of the lamp above Morton's bed. Pietje and I watch the stuff in the flask beginning to filter down the tube.

The guy tapes the needle onto Mort's arm and opens the valve. He checks the drip feed to be sure it's working and stands looking down at Mort for a while. Mort opens his eyes.

'Thanks.'

The blond guy goes out of the room without a word.

'Who was that man?' I ask when he's gone.

'You never saw him. He was never here.'

'OK. So what is it he's rigged up?'

'An intravenous solution of morphine sulphate. Someone will have to open the valve a little further every couple of hours. It'll take a while. I don't know how long. Why don't you go out and get us something to drink? Put on some music. Have a party.'

I fix the music, Led Zeppelin and that old stuff from the sixties which Morton likes, and Billy goes out to fetch some booze. Kip and Harko share a needle while Mort's on his morphine sulphate drip in the next room. Dad and Helen can't handle this. They leave their glasses untouched, sitting white and rigid beside Morton's bed and doing their vigil thing while the kids are getting stoned in the next room. Every couple of hours one of us goes in and opens the valve as Morton told us to do. I ask Mort if the music is OK and he says he can't hear it. He says to turn the music up and leave the door wide open, or at least I think that's what he says, because his speech is really slurred and he can hardly stay awake long enough to answer.

This is the last thing my brother said, or maybe he didn't, because he was slurring his words as he struggled to stay awake, and I'm just guessing what he might have said. Maybe I misheard what Morton said. At the time I think I hear him say to turn up the music and leave the door wide open, which is what I do, but later I'm not so sure, just as there'll be so many things I'm not too sure of after he's fallen into that deeper and deeper sleep, and just stops breathing some time around three o'clock in the morning.

SEVENTEEN

The autopsy is scheduled for 8 a.m., forty-eight hours after Morton dies. We're up the whole night, taking all kinds of stuff and telling ourselves it's to stay awake, but really it's to see us through this thing. Kip passes out and we have to leave him behind. It's just the four of us – Billy, Pietje, Harko and me – who finally make it to the hospital.

At the reception they tell us to go down to the basement, where we meet Dr Bloem, the pathologist who's going to be doing the autopsy. He's a pretty old guy, with white hair and a beard. He shows us some slides of cell tissues and stuff, talking in a really dry voice like he thinks this is not all that interesting himself, but it's kind of relaxing, the totally matter-of-fact way the guy puts himself across.

He asks if anyone has a question, and nobody does, so I ask him where Morton has been for the past forty-eight hours, and Bloem says here, they've had the patient here in the pathology department, but that's not what I wanted to know. I ask if Morton's body has had to be conserved some way. Bloem says the corpse has spent the intervening period 'in a refrigeration unit', i.e. in the ice box.

From the way Bloem uses words like 'deceased' and 'patient' I figure out there's a lot of etiquette surrounding an autopsy, because Bloem looks really uncomfortable when I mention Morton's name. He looks out of the window into the parking lot, and after a pause he says 'the corpse has been in a refrigeration unit', like he's teaching me the rules of the game. He repeats what I say, but using different words, like 'corpse' instead of 'body', eliminating the slightest personal trace. I go along with that. I appreciate how much easier it is to talk about these things.

After half an hour Bloem shows us out of his office and sets off down a corridor with the four of us in tow. Containers overflowing with hospital laundry line the walls. Bloem mutters something about overcrowding, and how bad it is that the pathologists have to compete with laundry people for space. He sounds apologetic, sort of ashamed it's so hole-in-corner the way they have to do their job.

We get to a junction of corridors, where people are wheeling laundry containers out onto a ramp and loading them into trucks, and it occurs to me this must be the reason why they have the pathology department down here. The undertakers can wheel the coffins out through the swing doors onto the ramp exactly the same way the laundry containers get taken out. I understand why Morton made his own arrangements to die at home. There's no difference between the way dirty laundry leaves the hospital to be washed and the way a dead body leaves it to be buried.

On coke I'm feeling cool and calm. I can see things like the logistics of laundry and corpses in a rational frame of mind. I see myself following Dr Bloem down these crowded, badly lit corridors, on my way to the autopsy that the pathologist is going to carry out on the deceased, and I can appreciate the rational order behind all of this without distaste or fear. I'm reassured by the total cool with which I'm going into this autopsy in accordance with Morton's, or rather, the deceased's last wishes.

Bloem pushes open a door and we find ourselves in a smaller corridor with more rooms leading off. I look into a lab, and an office, and then we're in a changing room where the walls are lined with shelves, containing piles of white linen. He tells us to take off our shoes and jeans, and gives each of us a stack of linen and a pair of white slippers. We put on these baggy white pants with strings to tie at the waist, white smocks, slippers and surgical gloves. Bloem tells us to take off our watches and jewellery. Then he disappears for ten minutes.

There's nowhere to sit down. We just stand and wait in this windowless room lined with shelves of white linen. Harko tells Pietje she looks neat in her outfit and Pietje thinks Harko looks great, too, but the truth is we don't look neat or great at all. We look jittery. We look like the bums we are, out of place in this medical gear, and I think how much more class those guys in the picture of *The Anatomy Lesson* had, with their ruffs and lace and pointed beards. We're one-dimensional cut-outs. There's no sense of mystery or wonder about us at all. We look like laundry people.

The pathologist comes back in and says they're ready to start if we are. He asks if everyone is OK and warns us we're here on our own responsibility. He looks round at us one by one, questioningly. We nod.

Bloem shows us out into the corridor and opens the door into the autopsy room.

It's a square white room with smoked glass windows. White and glass and steel, a functional coldness, is what the room says to you the moment you come in. Two stainless steel structures, the autopsy tables, stand in the centre of the room. They look like execution machines, the sort of thing you'd expect to find in a slaughter-house.

Right off I don't notice anything much else, just this dominance of polished, hungry steel. About a dozen people are standing around one of the autopsy tables where a shape lies covered with a white sheet. I mean, it's just a bundle, I don't pay too much attention to it. I see the white people. Most of them are students, wearing the same white pants and smocks and gloves that we are, but with Dr Bloem and two women and a thick-set guy with a black beard it's different, because these guys are wearing red gloves. There's this group of four red-handed people whom everyone else is gathered around, but what you notice is not all the whiteness there is in the room, the walls, the people and the sheet that you see when you come into the room. What you notice, what reaches out and grabs you, are these scarlet hands jumping out of all the whiteness. I can almost hear the colour scarlet, like a scream.

I'm sort of moving across the room with Harko and Pietje in the direction of the autopsy table, I don't know, there's something going on at a sink at one side, and I glance that way to see what's happening. For just a moment I'm distracted by what's happening at the sink, so it comes as a terrific shock when I turn back and look at the autopsy table to find that the sheet has gone and my brother Morton is lying there. The sheet is hardly off him when one of the women wearing red gloves starts briefing us on the clinical history of the deceased. I hear words like *cancer* and *pneumonia* and *refused any nourish-ment towards the end* through a screen of disbelief that it's Morton's body lying there, and that he's not going to get up off the table with a dead-pan face or pull any of his Buster Keaton stunts any more.

I'm looking at him in his deadness after a couple of days in the refrigerated room that have turned his skin a yellowish colour. He's lying stark naked on the table without anything to cover his genitals the way there is in Rembrandt's painting, and he looks just awfully vulnerable, with all these people standing round looking down at him. He's so distorted in death he looks as if his body is lying on two levels, his stomach flat and low and his chest grotesquely expanded, as if he'd taken one last gigantic breath that had never been exhaled. From the stomach down to his splayed feet he's flat and sunken, but that high, inflated chest looks somehow terrifically full of life. Mort's head is pushed back, covered with a mass of dark red hair that looks frozen, almost artificial, a part of him that looks young and vigorous, which death seems to have left untouched. His eyes are closed, his mouth open so that you can see the chipped corner of a front tooth, his head pushed back and exposing his throat exactly as if he were waiting to have it slit, and somehow I feel a special affection for that chipped tooth, remembering how it happened, and I begin to feel I made a big mistake in coming here as I grasp what's about to happen.

The autopsy table on which Mort is lying is tilted at a slight angle down towards the feet, *so that liquids can drain off,* is what I'm thinking, because the feet are lying in sort of a sink, and the feet look cold and vulnerable, all of him does, lying naked on that stainless steel, but somehow nowhere more so than his feet that lie splayed in the sink in a constant trickle of water. There's a bridge over his legs, fitted on top of the autopsy table just like you have over a bath-tub, and this bridge has kind of a draining-board, too, and sponges, and for a moment, absurdly, I think *Morton's in the bath-tub,* and these people are going to wash him. For a moment I'm hallucinating and seeing Morton stretched out in the bath-tub, waiting for Moo to come and sponge him. The guy with the black beard inserts a steel cushion under his neck to prop up the head, and I hang on to the idea that this is *to make him more comfortable*, until I see one of the red-handed assistants take a knife and hand it to Bloem.

The knife has a black handle and a short blade. It's shaped like an instrument for opening oysters. Bloem gestures with his hands as he's describing the anatomical procedure to the students, waving around the knife as he does so, and I just can't believe it, this man standing there and describing in cold blood how he proposes to cut the body open. I can feel my heart racing. All my instincts rush forward, cutting through the fuddle of coke and screaming inside me *what the fuck does this guy think he's doing?*

The pathologist inserts the knife into the left shoulder, just casually, and he draws it clean across the collarbone to the right, as if he were slicing through a strip of cork. Your eyes see this happen and your brain doesn't believe it. As you see this happen you don't believe that Bloem can stand there and casually cut Morton open with no one making any attempt to stop him. You wait for the door to burst open and someone to come rushing in to arrest him. You wait for the scream. You wait for blood to come pouring out. But there's no scream, no blood. All you see is the lining under the skin as the knife slices through a wad of yellowish, fatty tissue that rolls back and becomes visible under the incision. The pathologist makes a second cut from the throat to the groin. I look at this T-shaped cut across and down the body, with yellowish tissue bulging out exactly like foam rubber through torn upholstery. Bloem begins to peel the skin back.

I hear Pietje beside me hiss through her teeth. I look at her and Harko. I look at everyone standing around the autopsy table, with the same expression of utter fascination on their faces that you see in Rembrandt's picture, and inside me I hear Morton's voice as we stood looking at it in the museum in Den Haag. *You want to take the corpse apart and look inside.*

Bloem is peeling back the skin, and this is the point where I feel that maybe I'd do better to look away, but that I can't. Somewhere behind the horror there is the same fascination groping out of me that already has the others spellbound. I'm not seeing Morton any more. This atrocity is not being done to my brother. It's being done to someone else who bears a remote resemblance to my brother Morton, a clinical subject on the autopsy table, such a functional, impartially efficient machine that the body lying on it ceases to be a body and becomes flesh to be processed by the machine. The Morton I know ceases to be.

Standing silently round the autopsy table, it's like we are conspirators in some kind of atavistic ritual, allowing the subject on the autopsy table to be dehumanised so that our instincts can rush through the gaping wound that has been made in the body by the high priest's knife. I watch the rib-cage being exposed. I see the gristled rib-cage with bones gleaming white and lined with lean, reddish tissue, and already I'm thinking it looks hardly any different from the breast of a dismembered chicken. Dr Bloem hands a pair of shears to the thick-set, bearded man who is the lab technician. He cuts out the rib-cage, the shears making a crunching sound as they sever the bones on either side and along the top of the chest. The whole rib-cage is lifted out in a single piece and laid on one side, exposing the innards.

Suddenly there's an appalling smell in the room. It takes me a few moments to realise where it's coming from. The sharp, sour, extremely unpleasant stench is coming out of the inside of the corpse. It's the innards of the cadaver that stink. The skin is folded back, just like a shirt, over the sides and the arms and obscuring part of

102

the face. Once a body loses its wholeness you stop seeing it as a human being. You see it as another animal, crammed with sausage-like shapes in moist, transparent casings, and the bizarre thought passes through your head: all of this looks edible.

Bloem is rummaging with his red-gloved hands, detaching this mass of organs one by one, making little cuts through the white elastic film where they stick together, and the way he does this is not at all different from the kind of thing you watch over the counter in a butcher's store. He makes a third cut from the collarbone all the way up to the point of the chin, and folds the skin back in flaps that horribly remind me of the Peruvian cap my brother used to wear. The face is hidden under the flaps of skin. The body no longer has a face. What's lying here is just a piece of meat, and Dr Bloem is giving the students an anatomy lesson.

Two large, spongy masses on either side fill out the open chest cavity. They are the lungs. The pathologist draws our attention to their coarse-grained surface, mottled with dark stains. Someone asks him if they're nicotine stains. 'Coal dust,' he says, 'all of us look like that inside, because of the smoke and fumes and dirt in the air we breathe in our cities.' He begins to detach the lungs from the wall of the chest. They stick to the walls, and he has to reach in and pull them away from the ribcage with one hand while slicing away an adhesive film of skin with the other, explaining in his expressionless voice that the adhesion of the lung to the walls of the chest is a typical indication of pneumonia.

'Didn't you mention pneumonia in the patient's recent history?' he asks one of the assistants. She says she did, and Bloem nods as he lifts out the lungs and the heart in one piece, with the throat organs attached, and the tongue sticking out grotesquely at the top.

The tongue does it to me. I snap out of the clinical

103

thing I'd gone into like it was an anaesthetic. I know this tongue. You don't recognise a person's lungs and heart, but you've seen their tongue lots of times, and this is unmistakably Morton's tongue sticking out over the edge of the draining-board where Bloem has dumped the heart and lungs. I see Morton's tongue, and blood from his own heart and lungs dripping from the stainless steel draining-board onto the feet below as Bloem rinses them and begins dabbing them with a sponge. I edge away from the group and take out a handkerchief and pretend to blow my nose while I'm swallowing a handful of tranquillisers. I think maybe I should quit. I can't go through with this. Then I hear Bloem say in his steady voice, 'I think all of you can identify the disease of which the patient died. You can see the metastases at a glance. The tumours are not restricted to certain organs. The tumours have proliferated everywhere, clear indications of a global cancer in an extremely advanced stage, remarkable in a patient so young . . .'

I'm electrified. It's like ventriloquism. It's Morton's own analysis, delivered in the pathologist's voice. Morton's cancer is what I've come here to see.

Bloem doesn't seem to look for the tumours. He searches them out with the tips of his fingers. He invites the students to close their eyes and feel the tumours with their fingers. What you see are gristly, whiteish spots, calluses the size of large coins. There are tumours all over the lungs, around the throat and in the thyroid gland. The pathologist takes out the intestines in a second package. His fingers pry into them as he names the individual organs, liver, kidneys, pancreas, the compact dark mass of the lower intestines. There are tumours here, too.

I ask him where he thinks the cancer began. He says the body is so riddled with cancer it's impossible to say at this stage where it originated. He says histological analysis may later be able to clarify this, because cancer cells take on the structural characteristics of the organs in which they develop. 'Tumours found on the lung, but with cell structures characteristic of the thyroid gland, for example, would lead me to assume that was where they might have originated, spreading via the arteries to form metastases in other parts of the body.'

Perfectly relaxed, Bloem names the parts and describes how they all connect, just as if he was talking about a piece of machinery. He peels the organs out of their casings and holds them in the palm of his hand. He takes a foot-long knife and slices them in half. He hands specimens of these organs to the bearded technician, who places them in jars of formalin on the sideboard, and the autopsy room with all these jars and people walking back and forth in white smocks takes on the feeling of a bizarre kind of kitchen. It's somehow reassuring to have names and labels given to all these parts that are coming out, and to watch the way the pathologists cut off slivers and put them in jars. What started out as just a horrific mess is beginning to make sense to me. I'm feeling better. I'm getting on top of this thing. I must be, the kind of comparisons that start coming to mind. The slivers in the jars remind one of anchovies. You could say they look almost appetising.

Pietje has a hand covering her face. The foul smell is still hanging over the corpse. It's coming from the gall-bladder. It has a mottled dark green colour, covered with slime and what looks like algae, resembling something that might have come out of the sea. Bloem says the gall-bladder looks and smells this way because the deceased hadn't eaten in a long time. He says he's going to open the gall-bladder to take a look. He pricks it with the tip of his knife. A green-black liquid oozes out. There's such a horrible stench that I have to turn away.

The stocky guy with the beard is standing by the sink.

Inside the sink is Morton's heart. It's pretty weird seeing his heart in that sink. Suddenly I feel awfully weak. There's a chair in the corner where I sit down. I begin to feel faint.

The room is getting narrow and elongated and I'm looking at the heart in the sink like it was something at the end of a tunnel. There's the white of the sink at the end of the tunnel and the heart is there in focus. The arteries have been severed where they join the heart, leaving stumps that remind you of tubes coming out of an engine block. I watch the guy threading a piece of string through the openings into the heart. I ask him what he's doing. He says he's *stringing the heart out* so they can take a better look at it. The heart gets to be strung out on a wire frame and soaked in formalin, to harden the heart so they can cut it open and look inside without the view getting obscured by a deluge of blood. In an adjacent sink lies the lung. It looks enormous lying there. A pipe has been stuck into the lung, pumping in formalin to solidify it too, so they can cut into it when they start out on the histological analysis in a day or two. I'm taking in all these details. My mind is as sharp and precise as the pathologist's knife. I'm remembering all the things I'm seeing and hearing in the autopsy room as if my life depended on it.

When the tunnel disappears and the room is back in shape I get up and go over to the autopsy table. The pathologists are busy rinsing and stringing and pumping at sinks around the room. Harko and Pietje have left, and it's just Billy and the students looking down at the remains as Bloem is finishing the anatomy lesson. I look at Billy and remember he was a marine in Vietnam where he killed a lot of guys. He told me about it once down in Popeye's cellar. Killing those guys has left Billy really messed up. It's like he's gone into a trance. He's standing there with wide open eyes, absolutely motionless. The

106

students are stooping and peering as Bloem talks and points, but Billy's just rigid. I ask him if he's OK. He doesn't react. He's staring down at what's left on the autopsy table, like he was transfixed.

What's left is a shell with nothing in it, a sump that's been drained and cleaned out. Bloem is reaching into the sump. He pulls out the testicles from inside the scrotum like he's turning a sock inside out. He holds a testicle in the palm of his hand and slices it in half. A student holds up a jar and Bloem drops the two halves into the formalin solution. Then he picks up a saw.

He sets the saw cross-wise at the base of the spine and begins to saw. The saw rasps as it goes through the bone. He makes two diagonal cuts into the marrow of the spine, takes a hammer and chisel and knocks out a piece in the shape of a wedge. Someone hands him a nail-brush. Bloem holds the sample of spine in a bowl of water and brushes it. He picks it up for the students to see, a cross-section of the spine with the marrow and discs at intervals like some fibrous plant or a piece of bamboo. Bloem puts this in a jar, too. He pauses and looks down at the empty corpse.

What was inside the body now lies scattered all over the room, in sinks and bowls and on the draining-board. The pathologist looks around, taking stock of all these scattered pieces. I think that's it, he says at last, and I look up and notice the clock on the wall. It's ten o'clock. The corpse has been dismembered and samples collected in jars within two hours. I can't believe it. I feel as if I'd been in this room for a week.

Something is still holding Bloem by the autopsy table. He shakes his head and mutters. He looks up at the circle of people around him and says, 'This man died when he was very young. But on the inside he doesn't look young at all. A body has two ages, the age you see on the outside, and the age that only a pathologist sees, on the inside. From the outside this patient was young, but from the inside he was already old. You won't often see a dissection that shows such a difference between a body's two ages.'

Bloem turns away and strips off his gloves and throws them in a bin at the door. He holds it open and follows me into the changing-room. We put on our clothes, and stuff the smocks and pants into the container for the dirty laundry. Then we go out and see more laundry containers trundling along the corridor to the ramp to be loaded into the trucks. On our way down here the pathologist had complained about having to share space in the basement with guys who handle dirty washing, as if he thought this was sort of a yucky arrangement, but after all I've seen it seems absolutely appropriate to me.

I ask him what will be done with the body.

'That's the lab technician's job. He sews the bodies up and they're left in the morgue to be collected by the undertakers.'

We're standing on the ramp, watching the truck drive away, when Bloem asks me if I'd mind him putting a personal question. I say I don't mind, and Bloem scratches his beard. He says it's pretty irregular for friends and relatives of the deceased to attend the autopsy. In fact he never heard it happened. He'd like to know why someone donating his body made it a condition of donation that friends and relatives should be allowed to attend.

I go, 'It's pretty complicated, Dr Bloem. You would have had to know Morton, and how things were between Morton and me, before I could begin to explain why—'

I just break off and begin to howl. It's like the colour of the gloves in the white room I'd managed to keep staunched inside myself had finally burst and was beginning to bleed out of me. The howl pours out of me like a flow of blood. It's the scream I heard that wasn't there.

The scream is tapped in a vast reservoir, an endless geyser that pours and pours on out of me. It doesn't stop. I keep on hollering. I stand on the ramp and drown the whole parking lot with my hollering.

This Bloem guy, he's really nice. I mean, a guy like Dr Bloem must have seen an awful lot, he's an experienced and really human person. I guess he's been keeping tabs on me, and somehow he's been expecting this. He's not the dry old medical he pretends to be, he puts his arm round me and lets me holler, and then he squeezes, and keeps on squeezing until gradually I dry up and the hollering stops. We walk around the parking lot for a bit, and then we go into the canteen and have a cup of coffee, which is pretty much the way the Dutch react when they have any sort of problem on their hands. It sounds kind of bone-headed, the way the Dutch are, but give someone a cup of coffee and talk to them, and it's incredible how it can help. I wish I'd had a dad who'd been more like this Bloem guy.

When he says goodbye he gives me his card and tells me to call him if I ever feel the need to talk to him some more. I'm thinking it doesn't make an awful lot of sense to open up someone's dead body in order to find out about his life, and maybe this is why there's a sense of dissatisfaction after an autopsy, a feeling that whatever you might have been looking for, it has eluded you, but I don't tell Dr Bloem that. I just shake his hand, and head back home.

EIGHTEEN

It's three years since Morton died and things haven't changed too much. I guess the glaciers must still be receding. I'm on welfare. Holland is as flat as ever. They say there are mountains some place down in the south, but I don't know, I never got that far. I'm into *small* thrills, right? Like at the moment I'm in Amsterdam Central, feeding coins into the slot of the cigarette automate and waiting to see if anything will come out of the machine. Then I hear the *thtonk* as a packet comes down the chute, and when I put my hand in and touch the cellophane I feel a kind of relief. It's not an addiction thing. The machine has responded. It recognises I'm there.

I cross the station hall and see Pietje sitting on the floor under the neon signs above the meeting point. I do a little break-dance routine, imitating the dancing silhouettes in the neon sign overhead. Pietje watches me and smiles. She's happy to see me, I guess. Either I make Pietje quarrel or make her laugh. If we could do something about the area in between we'd have a relationship large enough to really live in.

While I'm doing my imitation of a dancing neon silhouette, Pietje sits on the station floor doing her imitation of a bag lady. Since she got back from New

York it's improved a lot. The details she's picked up look authentic. Like the tatty black dress she's worn for the past couple of months. Or the grime she allows to collect under her fingernails for a couple of days. Or the bag. Never any half measures with Pietje. She's brought along a large grey plastic sack, the kind you put out on the street for the trash collectors.

We get on a train and ride for an hour until we're way out in the country. Pietje's dad hasn't shown up to meet us. Typical. One of the few useful things the guy can still do with his MS is drive. There's no bus, needless to say.

We check out the bicycle sheds behind the station. I take out a few bikes and try running starts, jumping onto the bike in motion and jamming on the brakes to see if I can snap the lock. There's usually one where the run-and-jam technique works, but no free bike today. So we set off down the road and Pietje thumbs a lift.

A car stops with these two old numbers from the south of Holland in their holiday hats. We get into the car and for ten minutes become part of somebody else's life. The car is a living-room, packed with inflatable rubber toys and stuff, and we crowd in and become more of the holiday gear, yackering away non-stop. Nothing outside of the living-room exists. We're so nice and friendly and holidayish – it's all very *gezellig*. Ideally, one would never have to get out of strangers' holiday cars. In an ideal life one would step off one magic carpet onto another, packed with inflatable rubber toys, and just take off.

They let us out at the corner. I light a cigarette. Pietje drags the sack along behind her. We set off down a road with dinky sort of clapboard houses on one side overlooking the dunes on the other. The dunes stretch to the horizon. I can smell the sea.

The old guy is lying in a deckchair in the little garden in front of the house. He hears the sound of the sack dragging on the pavement and opens his eyes.

111

'Washing?'

'Uhm. Mother inside?'

'She'll be back later.'

Pietje kisses her father and takes the grey sack into the house. But for her laundry every couple of weeks, what would she need to come home for? I feel Cees's cheek against mine, the dry, papery feel of his skin. His eyelids hover for a moment against the brightness, and close again. His papery white arms lie on the chair-rests, palms upward. He's an old lizard sunning in the garden.

'Well, Kiddo . . . shall we go to the beach?'

'Sure.'

I go 'sure', like well-oiled and totally casual. Actually I'm pretty surprised. I never heard he got down to the beach. He must be feeling in good shape. I mean, I could go, 'Wow, the beach – think you'll make it, buddy?', which would be the honest thing to say if that's what's going through your mind. But that's not how we talk to people like Pietje's father. We go all casual and stuff, and pretend we're looking the other way. Pietje's father contracted MS fifteen years ago, when he was in his early thirties, and looking the other way has been pretty much the story of Pietje's life.

The funny thing with these MS guys is that you're not so much helping them get along as doing your damnedest to hold 'em back. It's like Cees can't put one foot in front of the other unless he's going hell for leather. Pietje and I take him between us, an arm round our shoulders, and do our damnedest to hold him back as he breaks into this pounding lurch.

His legs are going in all directions at once. He lunges along at this crazy pace because the moment he stops moving he's going to seize up and keel over. As we usher this erratic spasmobile through neat little seaside town streets I catch sight of poles standing to attention in front gardens, flying the Dutch flag horizontally in the wind, I mean ridiculous, as if they were all out there to salute or something, and I'm conscious of the boniness of Cees all the way up one side of me, and of the heat of his exertion, going out of him in great bounds.

'Some time since I . . . humph! . . . great day for the beach.'

Yeah, *great* day if we get there.

We reach the end of the dam and look down over the crowded golden Saturday strand.

A long flight of stairs leads down. Through Cees's eyes I look at this scene and eliminate everything but the essential. All he needs to see is that flight of stairs with its enabling railing, his passport to the beach. It's as if the scene had been appropriated by Christo for a variation of the running fence. Landscape with Railing, miles of beach empty of anything but a railing running on and on and disappearing over the horizon. Cees unlinks his arms and takes hold of Christo's landscape. Pitching forward, he grabs the railing. He descends the stairs in one gulp, an extraordinary upheaval of jerks, and disintegrates at the bottom. We prop him up again and support him to the nearest beach chair, his legs trailing limply through the sand.

'. . . Legs won't . . . legs any more . . .'

He bangs his head on the sunshine hood and groans. Pietje unfolds towels. I head for the kiosk to get some beer. There's not any hurry about this. We're going to let things settle. We're going to let things regroup and slowly get back to normal again.

If it were my disease, I'd want to talk about it. I'd want to listen to me. It would be the most interesting copy I had. Everything absolutely familiar, everything absolutely different. Take coming down those stairs. We don't even think about it. But Cees just ran a marathon backwards, standing on his head. I mean, for him it was a hell of an accomplishment getting down those stairs.

113

I'd talk about my vision of an endless railing disappearing over the horizon. But people like Pietje's father live in *spite* of their disease. They don't seem to want to live *with* it. Fact is they do live with it, only they act like they don't. They act as if it wasn't there.

I can't overlook that something of this attitude has rubbed off on Pietje and her mother. They've spent so much of their lives dodging this invisible companion of Cees that it can sometimes seem they weren't there either. Pietje started going into the unobtrusive mode as soon as she got to the house. She's in it now, wearing a black swimsuit, dead silent on a beach chatty with colours. She's holed up in Patrick Süskind's book *Perfume*, right in the shade.

'Sometimes it's there in a sentence,' muses Cees apropos nothing particular in the landscape, almost as if he'd latched on to what I was thinking about Pietje, 'in just a few words.'

I hand him a can of beer.

'Oh? Was there something you had in mind?'

'A melody. You come across it in a book, and it's humming a couple of notes that matter to you.'

'I think we should move the things up the beach, Cees. The tide's already nibbling at my towel . . . how about your chair?'

'That'll be OK for a while.'

I pick up the stuff we've scattered around us and carry it up the beach. I make conversation with the old boy to keep him happy.

'How does the melody sound?'

'It sounds like something inside you. It may be insignificant in itself. It's what it can trigger inside you.'

'For example?'

'Examples only disappoint. Examples sound banal. They are banal. But what do they set off, those flocks of birds that rise in a white swarm from the square,

114

inspiring in Thomas Mann a sense of something he describes as a light, festive beauty?'

'I don't know, Cees. What do they?'

'You stand in the cool of the morning in a strange city. You feel a draught, of the cool before the heat, perhaps of excitement, mingled with the buzz of traffic, the medley of different voices, smells and . . . just ordinary things like that. The excitement always gives way to resignation. The sensation in the end is always one of loss. That's a melody.'

'Who else is there?'

'No one that matters to me. It's the sound of my own extinction, you see.'

'But there must be others.'

'Others?'

'Other melodies.'

'There are others, oh yes.'

He doesn't sound too convinced.

Pietje and I go for a swim. We swim out only fifty yards or so and are already separated from the beach by a grey expanse. We turn and swim back at the same time, sensing the sea's hostility.

The sea creeps up the shore. Cees lunges and sways, dragging the chaise longue, a blue-and-white striped dragon, behind him up the beach. We plunge out, dripping like labradors, Pietje in her glistening black skin, and scoop up our books, beer cans and sunglasses, flotsam it seems has been deposited on the fringe of the tide.

Then it's nice for a while. You could say things are pretty near perfect. We're on a magic carpet called Steenhoven beach. Pietje lies reading on the sand. On the edge of her silence I can tell it's becoming a silence of content. Cees and I look out to sea. I fold my arms behind my head and squint past the beer can, a lighthouse looming on my stomach, at the far side of the horizon a thousand miles away.

115

'Damn sea . . .'

The tide has a go at Cees's chaise longue, making slurping sounds as it sucks at the wheels. Somehow this interruption is final. OK, so the sea doesn't want us on the beach. We head for home, Cees pitching right into the stairs and mounting the dam in a frenzy.

Pietje's knickers are waving enthusiastically on the washing line. Hi, folks! Hi there! It's more of that flag language in front gardens, this time signalling that Pietje's mother's back home.

She smiles, makes tea and puts out cake. She brushes strands of hair out of her eyes. Pietje's mother has that faded look of having been through the wash too many times.

The talk meanders amiably. Pietje coils a hair round a finger, smiling absentmindedly. Her mother switches on the lamp and begins to fold Pietje's washing. Pietje puts it back in the grey plastic sack. Her father has taken out a Chinese primer from college days in search of some character he has forgotten and can't find.

I stand out on the porch smoking, watching the night stretch out in the sky above the dunes. When I come back into the room Pietje is talking about opening a chain of laundromats in New York, or New Orleans, she's not yet sure which. Her mother sits perfectly motionless with folded hands. The sack bulges on a chair by the open door, the neck throttled with twine.

When I say goodbye my fingers rest momentarily on the back of Cees's skull, and against my face I still feel the surprise of the stubble on the dry-as-dust parchment of his skin as I walk out of the house.

NINETEEN

There's just blueness without a sky. It's one of those blue evenings without even a chip at the edges.

On the sleeve of the record I draw two lines of coke. I sniff up mine and hand the sleeve to Pietje. It's an old Led Zeppelin album, plastered over with all that wonky wavy psychedelic stuff from the sixties.

I sit on the floor with my legs stretched out, propping myself up on my arms. I can feel sand in the wrinkles of my elbows. I peel my eyes and keep absorbing blueness, and I guess Pietje does, too. We're both naked at room temperature of 25°C, with the benefit of natural air-conditioning, a slight chill factor that's extremely pleasant, just under the open window. I watch Pietje's shoulders turn blueish. Come over here, blue ivory, is what I'd like to say, but my lips don't manage the effort.

Blue ivory comes over without my having to say it.

She straddles my lap and combs my hair with her fingers. I draw up at the smooth blue hearth of Pietje's body. I can feel myself frosting all over, reverse engineered into some semi-solid state, a frosty anaesthesis of arousal. She takes me inside her blue tent. With her fingertips and her nipples she grazes my chest, and where she does I feel a darker blue well sluggishly out of a lacework of wounds.

Transfixed – maybe for ten minutes, maybe for two hours, my chin propped on her shoulder, waiting for the guillotine to come down.

'Why does it have to be *that* melody?' Pietje asks at last. 'Why does it have to be the sound of his own extinction?'

I float on up and up, sustained by her question mark. Nice place, interesting shelves with jars whose labels I try to read as I float on past. Seems I must be coming up where Alice in Wonderland went down. I'm reluctant to get into this grown-up talking thing, highly reluctant.

'I guess that's Papa's theme park, honeysmacks. Same with Morton, only your papa's dying an awful lot more slowly.'

'I'm sick of it.'

Another hour goes by. Blue recedes, the defrost comes on.

Slowly I come out of Pietje's tent and make some coffee. A full moon stands enormous at the window and pours into the apartment. It's so bright I haven't realised we've been sitting there without lights on. Stark naked in the blue moonlight, Pietje reaches up to one of those shelves and takes the jar down.

We sit at the kitchen table drinking coffee. Cups, sugar and condensed milk crowd the edges. In the space in the middle is the jar containing what I think must be my brother's brain. The whole room is blue-lit with a soft splash, almost a breeze of moonlight.

Pietje picks up the jar and gives it a shake. Conserved in methyl alcohol, Morton's brain bobs up and down inside the jar in slow motion.

Pietje gets up, collects more jars from the shelves and stacks them on the kitchen table. Inside their jars they all do their slow-motion, methyl alcohol dance – Morton's liver, kidneys, pituitary, testicles, heart, lungs writhing on the kitchen table in the breeze of moonlight.

'Be a good girl and put them *very carefully* back where you found them.'

'No.'

Pietje lights a cigarette and comes and sits on my knee. She hands me the cigarette.

'The jars must come down from those shelves, Kiddo.'

'Why?'

'Some time they'll have to come down.'

'They're souvenirs.'

She gets up. 'I'm sick of it. I can't bear it any more. All these ghouls –'

I sit and smoke.

Pietje moves around the room, picking things up, dropping them, picking them up again and putting them on, half-wittedly getting dressed.

'Please stay.'

She stands behind me, her hands heavy on my shoulders.

'When are you going to bury him, Kiddo?'

It must already have been light when I fell asleep, but I didn't hear the door when Pietje left, don't have any recollection of her going home at all.

TWENTY

I'm waiting at the street corner when Harko comes out of the Shell building. He stops to chat with a group of guys at the entrance. They all look pretty much alike in their suits and ties. You can tell Harko apart from the others because he stands out in the crowd on account of his white-blond hair, but otherwise he looks like all the other Shell guys. Hell, at the moment he *is* a Shell guy. I watch him cross the parking lot and get into one of the delivery trucks with SHELL written across the sides.

The truck roars out of the gate and screeches to a halt at the corner. Harko leans out and looks me over as if he's astonished to find me there. It must have to do with the way his eyebrows wander high up his forehead. He has this look of permanent surprise on his face.

'Wotcher,' he goes, 'like *your* knickers. Leather?'

'Plastic. What's this truck deal?'

'Company car. A fringe benefit, innit.'

He opens the door and I hop up into the cab.

Harko speaks Cockney overlaid with a Dutch accent. It sounds a bit phoney, but it's not, just how a Dutchman learns English when he's lived in the east end of London. He talks in a round sort of way, pursing his lips, like he had something hot in his mouth. It can sound pretty arch.

'We now proceed south-east to premises in the vicinity of Zeedijkstraat. Am I right, Kiddo? Wasn't this the plan?'

Harko leans on the wheel, laughing soundlessly inside himself. I don't get the point. It doesn't worry me. Probably there isn't a point to be got. There's a streak of mental illness in the family that occasionally shows up in Harko.

Harko is taking off his tie. I snap open the locks on the black attaché case lying on the seat and look inside. It's empty.

'Why bother with an attaché case if you don't carry anything in it?'

'Because you can't see that on the outside, can you.'

'So what?'

'So that's a philosophy of life, innit. Hold the wheel just a mo.'

I hold the wheel as Harko takes off his jacket and trousers.

'Do us a favour and hang that lot up, will you, before it gets crumpled.'

'Hang it up where?'

'I wouldn't be at all surprised if there's a hanger or two in the back.'

I squeeze between the seats into the back of the truck. There are piles of cartons marked SHELL, but also a clothes stand with half a dozen outfits hanging on it, and a mattress strapped to the side of the truck.

'Hey, this is pretty neat.'

'It's where I'm living at the moment. It's the outer fringe benefit, innit. For homeless Shell employees.'

'You *live* in this thing?'

Harko does his mirthless laugh, this time out loud.

'Ever hear of our world-famous spy force? I'd like to have been a spy. The double life, eh, Kiddo? Me and someone else who looks just like me. The doppelgänger routine. I'm good at that. But in Holland there's not much demand for spies. You have to work for Shell instead.'

'But what d'you actually do?'

'You frig around. You do fuck all.'

We get to the Nieuwe Markt and Harko parks the truck in a sidestreet. An African is leaning against the wall with his eyes shut. I can only make out the word DAMN on the logo on his baseball cap because the rest of it is turned to the wall. I'm compulsive about logos. If I see one I have to read it. I'm wondering whether to ask the guy for a cigarette so that I can read the rest of his logo when Harko jumps out of the back of the truck and slams the doors shut.

This Harko is a different guy. The guy who came out of the Shell building stays locked up in the truck. His doppelgänger is wearing jeans, a T-shirt and a bomber jacket with rips along the sleeves. We turn the corner where two Asian girls are standing in topless bikinis in a box window, so motionless you look twice to check if they're real, with these bored-as-hell expressions on their faces as Madonna comes blasting out of the entrance. Harko goes into overdrive and dives through the doorway like he's desperate. Probably he was popping pills to kick off before he left the Shell building.

We hit this barrage of noise and then a counter in semi-darkness. A black guy Harko seems to know is sitting there on a bar stool in sunglasses. They trade a few punches and go through a palm-slapping routine like volleyball players do when they won the point. It looks so stagey it kind of embarrasses me. I watch them do this weird conversation with the smash-volume Madonna soundtrack superimposed on top of pictures in which two guys are talking at the same time and you can't make out a word they're saying. You watch their lips move but all you hear is *Frankie* and *spanky* coming out of their mouths in Madonna's voice. The black guy reaches under the counter and pulls up cans of beer. Harko gulps down a can at one go. The black guy doesn't drink. He just sits there in his dark glasses looking cool. Harko zaps a second beer while I'm still sipping my first. It seems to be an either-or thing in here, I mean, *sipping* feels like it's bad style. Girls in these places want to get on with it and take their money. The black guy looks like he never sipped anything in his life.

Harko snaps into action. One of the girls steps out of her window like she'd suddenly come to life and follows him upstairs. Harko taps his watch and holds up five fingers before he disappears. This gets me involved. I think this is vaguely interesting. I press the stop-watch button on my Citizen, under the counter, so the black guy doesn't see what I'm doing, and I'm still doodling patterns in the moisture on the side of the can when Harko comes down again, and I stop my watch at five minutes and twenty seconds. There's more palm-slapping stuff between Harko and the other guy, and I notice Harko slips him a package that isn't money. Exit.

'Eat,' says Harko, hitching his pants with just a touch of swagger.

I go, 'So how was the spanky?'

Harko stops and looks me over.

'Know what you are? A filthy dirty voyeur, that's what you are.'

'I'm not a performing animal. I don't mix money and sex.'

'It's an unhealthy attitude. Of course you're a fucking performing animal.'

'Not in five minutes twenty seconds.'

'That was only because her handkerchief got caught in my zip.'

I grimace.

'That makes it even worse. Just disgusting.'

'D'you think she'd prefer it to take ten minutes? My bit of dribble. Or half an hour? My little friend, you amaze me. Do you know what you're going to do this evening?'

'Tell me.'

'You're going to smoothtalk a girl in a bar or somewhere and have sex with her—'

'Whuuh.'

'—under false pretences, telling her all sorts of lies when all you're after is a bit of dribble. Now that's what *I'd* call immoral and disgusting behaviour.'

'Girls in bars know that, and you know they know, and neither of you lets on. It's a game, Harko. I have a manual back home which is all about the mating rituals of performing animals. I'll lend it to you some time. Because you don't know about games, you're such a dumb prick—'

Harko takes a swipe at me which I see coming a mile off, and I duck, casually.

'—that you have to pay for it, because there's nothing like a nice wholesome business transaction to make sex legit. I mean, you don't even *know* the size of the hang-up you're into.'

'Bugger off.'

'Turn around and have a look at it, this red light district, crawling with businessmen who know everything about deals and nothing about games, because deals square consciences and you have your bit of dribble and go home as if nothing happened, which makes this liberal thing just total crap, it's not liberal, what this town respects is *mercantile*.'

'Not bad, not bad. For an imitation.'

Harko stops at a kebab stand and delves into his pocket as he socks it to me on the jaw.

'You're beginning to sound like Morton.'

I'm pretty sensitive about being told I'm like Morton.

In fact it irritates me like hell. Harko knows this, which is why he's not letting go.

'Game, Kiddo. You like games. Like to play a game? This one's called home truths and no prisoners taken. You know what held Morton back?'

'What d'you mean, held him back?'

'All those places Morton was going but never went. You did. You held him back.'

Harko's dragged me into this conversation, always lurking when he's around, of life-and-death importance to me, which I dread and which at the same time fascinates me, and which I'm having to make a physical effort to square up to while Harko's fiddling around with small change and then angling at the skewer for a nibble without getting sauce down his shirt. It's extremely frustrating. I square back down again and stand at ease, because anything of vital importance I'm going to say will feel like an interruption of someone more interested in eating a kebab.

'Morton had this brother', goes Harko between mouthfuls, 'who never got round to being anything much but a hanger-on, conning hand-outs disguised as welfare from the rest of us mercantile fellow taxpayers, and fancying that was pretty clever. Am I wide of the mark?'

'Way off.'

'OK. Morton may have been bright, but he wasn't streetwise like his brother. He didn't have the equipment. By our standards he was a pushover, a softy. But a good bloke.'

Harko wipes his fingers on a paper napkin and tosses it into the trash can.

'By the way. Before I forget. The little goodies you've been waiting for. Only came in this morning. This is A1 coke, Kiddo, new product line, back of a Guatemalan lorry. Here.'

'How much?'

'Free sample. Keep the clients happy.'

'Wow. Thanks.'

'Let's go and have a smoke.'

Harko lays an arm round my shoulder, leaning on me just a little as we walk back down Zeedijkstraat. We turn down the street where the Shell truck is parked, and while Harko's getting his cigarettes out of the truck I notice the African in the baseball cap. He's moved across the road and given himself a change of walls. He's leaning against the No Parking wall on the other side. The guy's far out on some trip and still has a long way to come down. I get the rest of the logo as we walk past, which reads DAMN, I'M THE BEST, and I think if you saw that in a movie it would seem so corny you just wouldn't believe it.

This area around Zeedijkstraat is full of corny things you wouldn't believe if you saw them in movies. It's not an area I like too much. It's full of people who've lost control over their lives, which is why they keep on getting themselves into situations that strike you as corny as hell because outside the Zeedijkstraat area they're so improbable. But inside the Zeedijkstraat area *life is incredibly corny.* It's full of people who see themselves as tragic figures, ham actors acting out soap-opera lives. There's no way you can put Zeedijkstraat on screen, because the people there do such a lousy imitation of life nobody would believe you. While Harko and I are walking past lousy imitations of life I really dig down into it and ask myself: why is this? And the answer I come up with is that people get themselves into these corny situations you wouldn't believe if you saw them in a movie because they're ham actors in the first place. Only a ham actor would go on the set in Zeedijkstraat with a logo like DAMN, I'M THE BEST wrapped around his head. It's asking for trouble. The guy's on the trash pile and nobody gives a shit because they know he needn't be, the *uitcaring* people are waiting off set with welfare cheques and welcoming arms. Since the welfare office set up in Amsterdam, soap opera has taken over and real life has gone out of business. This is what's weird about the place. Nothing matters. The *uitcaring* services have nursed real emotions to death.

'Where's the risk in it for *you*?' goes Harko as we hit a terrific crowd packing Voorburg Wal. I listen to Harko bragging about how he operates without a safety net and think he's talking crap, everyone in this village is doing their own high-wire act while the welfare people are holding out rubber sheets and looking up with smiling faces. Go on, jump. It doesn't hurt. Look, *I'm* the honest guy, *I* know this isn't for real.

The crowd sucks us in, a tongue that hangs out panting all the way down Voorburg Wal and greedily sucks us in. We swell the crowd and become part of its greed. My shoulder's gone numb where Harko's leaning on it, and what looked like a friendly, kind of a protective gesture when he first put his arm round me is beginning to feel like he's pushing me down. I feel like the next midget in line, recruited along with the Heinekens and the topless girls as part of Harko's supporting cast. Almost every store window we pass seems to be stacked to the ceiling with whips, dildoes and sex mags, you feel beaten up just noticing this stuff and I'm wondering who *buys* it all as we peel off from the crowd and sidetrack, inevitably, into Popeye's.

TWENTY-ONE

Ceremoniously we enter on the first beat of the Water Music, grinding out of the woofers in bands of bright metal I can almost reach out and touch. The Indonesian clique is in place, glittering with their jewellery, their blondes and their mastiffs. Eustace holds court on a bar stool in front of the counter. Eustace owns Popeye's. He clears more than five thousand a month. He's a little rat of a guy and five thousand a month makes him even worse. He perches on this high stool, wearing a three-piece suit and holding a bulldog with a studded collar on a leash as he taps his feet in time to George Frederick Handel.

'Hey, guys! Hey, *Kid*do, where you bin?' goes Eustace, slithering down and coming forward all phoney smiles and flickering eyes. Eustace has a way of slithering all over the rotten furniture in Popeye's that reminds you of a rodent gliding around a trash heap. He doesn't come up much higher than my shoulder. I look down into a dark, pitted face with quick eyes you can never pin down for a second.

'That's a pretty neat tie, Eustace,' I go, making an effort to be friendly for as long as Eustace's bulldog is sniffing my genitals, but his eyes have already taken me in and flickered past to Harko. I hop up into place beside the girl sitting next to Eustace at the counter. It's murky in Popeye's, I mean it's like sitting in a cave where the tribe has been cooking, it's foggy and dark as hell, but when this girl turns round to look at me the photon level picks up dramatically. This is the lightest, whitest blonde girl I ever saw. We move straight out of solar eclipse into broad daylight. I'm stunned.

'Wow! How did you do that?'

'How did I do what?'

'The way you switch on the light. That's quite something.'

She smiles and frowns at the same time. It's very becoming. This girl looks like she's sixteen and just a tiny bit. Her skin is so pale it looks like it's never been used. Eustace intervenes, his claw on her shoulder. My protective instincts are immediately aroused.

'You guys want something to drink? Beer? Coke? Ashok, get her a Coke and tell her about India. She wants to know about India.'

Eustace slithers downstairs with Harko. I watch them go into the converted toilet Eustace calls his office.

Ashok is Popeye's galley-slave. He's stirring grass into a saucepan of milk, his back to the counter, and without turning round he goes, 'What do you want to know about India?' in this gloomy, really weary voice, like he's asking about ships and tonnage and miles left to row. I mean, it finishes India off completely. As a subject of conversation, India sinks and goes straight to the bottom. The girl is speechless.

She turns to me for help.

'Are you and Eustace friends?'

'Not exactly. You see, I'm employed by the municipality.'

She nods. This radiant sixteen year-old is bright. She's taken the irony in her stride a lot quicker than I meant it.

'You mean you live in Amsterdam?'

'That's right. And you? You're . . .'

I'm about to say Finnish, but somehow it doesn't sound right to ask someone if they're Finnish. It sounds kind of insulting.

'. . . from Finland?'

'Sweden.'

My geography comes in more or less on cue.

'Helsinki?'

She smiles a little thinly.

'I think I mean Stockholm. From Stockholm?'

'From Jokkmokk.'

The photon level instantly goes down. It's a funny thing with Scandinavian girls. I mean, this kind of thing has happened to me before. You're in the middle of a friendly conversation when they turn on you and say *Jokkmokk* right out of the blue, and things start going downhill.

She goes, 'You don't *look* like you're employed by the municipality.'

'Exactly. That's because . . . look, this is confidential. Would you mind leaning this way a bit? That tall guy I came in with, the tall blond guy in the leather jacket, you know, with torn sleeves, looking a real bum . . .'

I'm murmuring into her ear and sniffing this cool scent, kind of forest and white water, a fresh-air tang, boy this is *health*, inhaling it bushelwise from the pale blonde hair she pushes back from her forehead and holds in a bunch.

'Well, he's an undercover agent. We're . . . aaaah!'

'What?'

'I mean, he and I are from the narcotics squad.'

'But it's legal,' she goes in this stage whisper, 'they even have it on the menu. They don't have anything *else* on the menu. You know, some Japan*ese* tourists were in here a minute ago, and imagine what.'

'What?'

'They asked for a cup of *coffee.*'

'Jeeks.'

'Well, it is a coffee house. But Eustace said no, they didn't serve coffee alone, only with a side order of marijuana. He said either you smoke pot or you leave. So they did.'

'Smoke?'

'Leave. They were awfully confused.'

'Bet Eustace didn't tell you to leave.'

'I wanted to talk about India.'

'Eustace isn't from India. He's Indonesian. He's never been to India in his life. Tell me . . . do you use some kind of, you know, like aerosol?'

'I beg your pardon?'

I glance over my shoulder and see Eustace and Harko closing the deal.

'Look, I don't want you to fall into their clutches. Upstairs it's a regular coffee house, but that's just a front. The bad things go on downstairs. Heroin traffic. White slave trade. Don't turn round. Any moment now there's going to be a raid. I want you to get up casually and leave. Walk out the door and don't look back. Don't get involved in this thing. For your own sake. Please.'

I can be a pretty persuasive talker, because I know how to finetune feedback into the loop. To persuade a person you have to use their own responses against them. When I'm talking to a girl I watch her face closely to track my flight path. I make adjustments according to what I see. I can see Northern Lights still flickering when I tell her not to get involved. Maybe too stern. It's not until I ambush her with that *please* that I get the bleep, and know I'm on target.

She finishes her Coke and does sort of a yawn, showing a set of spruce-bark white-water molars flawlessly in

131

place. I want to say goodbye but that would be conning myself, I mean a hundred percent Zeedijkstraat corniness. Instead I look into her mouth and think: this girl has a future in dental advertising. She gets up. She walks to the door and doesn't look back. She's *perfect.* I see her in the crowd and then she's gone.

Eustace opens the office door. Just great timing. I hop off the stool and sidle downstairs. I stand over the pool table and slide balls over the baize while he and Harko are chatting. I slide a couple and then I hurl them. The first ball goes *zonk* into the corner pocket, and Eustace goes *chattery-chat,* and the next one goes *crrunch,* flies off the table and hits the wall. Eustace turns round with flickering tongue and snakey eyes.

'Hey man, what the fuck are you doin'? That's a *pool* table, OK?'

'Sure.'

He slithers back upstairs. I take a cue off the wall and set up the balls on the table while Harko's making a phone call in the office. The Indonesians and Surinams with dreadlocks and albino mastiffs squatting at their heels are sitting frozen in the gallery over the pool table, staring out into the street exactly as they were when we came in. They're all stoned. They sit up there like effigies carved out of a cliff. They don't even hear what Eustace is saying.

'Hey, where did that blonde go?'

Downstairs Harko's still on the phone and I'm taking my time setting up the balls on the pool table.

'Hey, Ashok! Where the fuck did that girl go?'

'I've no idea. She just went.'

'Didn't you talk to her about India?'

'She didn't want to talk about India.'

'You stupid fucker!'

Harko comes out of the office and I stop pretending I'm going to play pool and follow him downstairs into the cellar. There's all this junk down in the cellar, broken furniture and bicycle wrecks. The whole place smells of urine and mould. Harko pushes the door open at the end of the passage.

A young guy is lying on a mattress. The cellar in Popeye's is where effigies go when they can no longer stand. His eyes are fixed on the ceiling, I mean just rigid with this stare. He's a nice-looking kid, and it's a pity, because you can see he's deep into training for a classic Zeedijkstraat role. 'Silly bugger,' goes Harko, prodding the guy with his foot. We sit down on the beat-up sofa with one end missing and look at the kid on the mattress as we fix our bazookas. I never allow myself to get depressed, I just don't ack*nowledge* it until I see it in the size of the coke line I've laid out on the mirror, and by that time lift-off is just a snort away.

'What's the movie, then?' goes Harko, lighting up as I do my mega-snort. 'Fancy some action replay?'

We're into our old routine. He'll tell me whether I do or not. The sex action replay down in Popeye's cellar is getting to be a goddamn *ritual*. We're like two dirty old guys jerking off on this beat-up sofa with one end missing.

'Standing blow-job. I'm standing. She's kneeling. Get the picture?'

'Just about.'

'It's a tight shot. What they call a head shot.'

Harko, or the heroin he's smoking, reconsiders this.

'Actually, it's just lips and her nose and an *immense* cock.'

'Ah, now he must be new. This guy with the immense dick, I mean, he's not on your payroll, Harko. None of us have ever seen this—'

'It's in technicolor. Scarlet lips. White prick, blueish around the nostrils.'

'The what?'

'Soaring, whitest prick of sperm whale. Blueish blow-hole. It's wicked. Scarlet lipstick rings of somebody's suck marks.'

'Wow.'

'OK. Now what am I thinking? You're standing in the Shell building is what I'm thinking. You're talking to your boss. There's a meeting in his office. People from acquisition and logistics are there, secretaries in glasses and starched blouses, sitting with crossed legs in skirts. You're standing in the middle of the room with your knickers down.'

Harko exhales, and his words go trailing out smoke-wreathed, crumbling in the air.

'You've *exposed yourself.* That's what I'm thinking while I'm getting the blow-job in Zeedijkstraat.'

'You've blown it,' I suggest. Briefly my head has been wrapped in concrete, and now I'm clear of the concrete I'm incredibly on the mark.

'Exactly. Because this spy business,' goes Harko, 'it's sneaking upstairs and putting my mum's knickers on, innit, while she and Dad are watching telly and might come up any minute. It's all that rubbish, innit. Me and the doppelgänger and catch us if you can. We're a fuck-ing sex cartoon on a lavatory wall. That's why Marijke kicked me out.'

'Why?'

'Because that's the only way I can do it now. Standing in a bleedin' meeting in Shell with me trousers down. I'm trapped. You know something, Kiddo?'

'What?'

'I think that bloke lying over there is dead.'

We sit there for a while, looking at the guy on the mattress and wondering if he's dead.

I go, 'How d'you know if someone's dead?'

'They're dead when they stop ticking.'

Neither of us moves. I'm getting into a refrigerated

134

phase where the kid on the mattress feels like he's a mile away.

Harko pushes up his sleeve and scratches his arm.

'There's a room in that Shell building,' Harko goes, 'where they store platinum discs. I was in there once. Platinum discs. No idea what they're for. They're locked up in cabinets behind bullet-proof glass. I tapped the glass and the bloke in the room said it was bullet-proof. I asked him why, because who's going to shoot a platinum disc? The bloke said the platinum in those cabinets was worth more than the Shell building and everything in it.'

I go, 'This cellar's afloat.'

'I mean, Jesus fucking Christ. More than the—'

'We must be down to water level, Harko. I can feel the goddamn cellar rocking. We gotta get the kid outa here.'

I go over to the kid and start slapping his cheeks the way they do in movies. It works in movies. It doesn't here.

Harko gives me a hand. We get the kid to his feet and prop him up.

'He's ticking all right,' says Harko.

We walk the kid up and down and slap his face a bit more. The kid mumbles. We kind of push and carry him upstairs.

We've been down in that cellar for a couple of hours. It's around half past two. The effigies are still in place in the gallery, but another Indian is now on late shift behind the counter and Eustace has disappeared. We get the kid some coffee.

'You OK, kid?'

The kid nods.

'Where's Eustace?' demands Harko.

'He went home.'

'Leaving one of his customers unconscious in the cellar?'

135

The Indian shrugs.

'That's his business.'

'It *is* his business. Because one of these days there'll be someone lying dead down there and Eustace is going to find himself in big trouble.'

'Guy doesn't look too dead to me. Are you paying for his coffee?'

We look round and find that while we've been arguing with the Indian the kid has grown legs and taken off. We leave Popeye's in disgust. I don't much feel like going home. Harko doesn't have a home to go to. As the coke begins to wear off, I can feel myself going into defrost. The question I've so far managed to ward off is shaping up at the back of my head and I'm beginning to feel pretty uncomfortable. I pop an XTC and we head across town, and headless people who can change colour are already springing up and exploding around me by the time we hit Siberia. We slide into these deep lounge chairs in the corner under an awning of soft lights and soft music, and I see all these ghosts from the past showing up at the bar, and I hear myself asking Harko, 'How come you think I killed my brother Morton?'

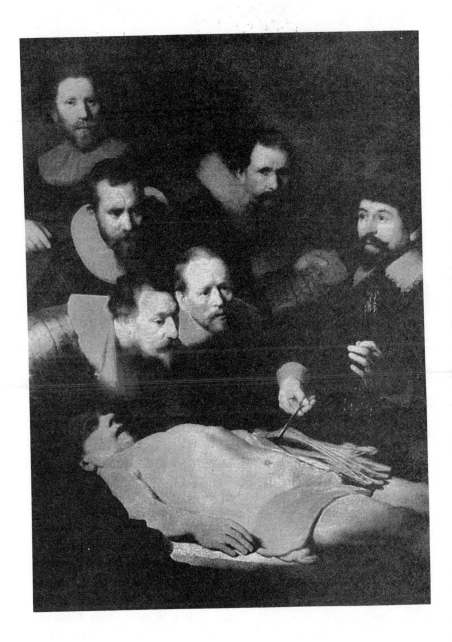

TWENTY-TWO

I guess one of the reasons why Morton sticks around is because I don't have answers to these questions. There's the question of the motives behind Morton's wish to have a group of friends *attend his autopsy*. And then there's the question of *why they agreed*. Even with Pietje I avoid this subject. Under the circumstances – he only had a few weeks to live, the wish on Morton's side took agreement on our side for granted – we didn't have an awful lot of choice. We felt we owed it to Morton to go along with this wish. That's OK, I mean, it'll do as an explanation. But for me this thing has to go deeper. There I am, standing in a group of people around Morton in his wheelchair, nodding and saying in as many words, sure, pal, we'll be there, and we're talking about being there for his dissection when he's dead, and the guy's my brother. Slumped in a chair in Siberia I watch all these ghosts show up at the bar, Harko and Billy, who were there and still are, and Morton and an exploding head called Kip who used to be there but no longer are. Kip OD'd and I've not seen him around Siberia for a while. He sat next to me in the back of the minibus when we drove to Den Haag. This was Morton's last outing. He was already pretty far gone, I guess, but he'd taken it into his head to make this trip to Den Haag. And it *was* a trip, with Billy's high-grade Indian tea doing the rounds and Morton insisting on taking a puff whenever the bazookas came his way and having himself, all things considered, a hell of a time.

We got to Den Haag and drove through the town and I think for the rest of us that was it, and we were ready to head right back to Amsterdam, except Morton, who wanted us to look at pictures in a museum. Morton couldn't make it round the museum on his own, so at the entrance we asked for a wheelchair. That's one of the great things about Holland. Wherever you are, if you need a wheelchair, they'll have one. They have wheelchairs everywhere, lined up under the starter's flag, as if expecting candidates for wheelchairs to descend *any minute*. We trooped into this museum, Billy, Harko, Pietje, Kip and me, with Morton on wheels, and it was kind of fun pushing him around the museum in a wheelchair. There was this scene in an empty hall with enormous pictures of fat women looking really gross in the nude where Kip and Billy started a tag game that involved Morton's chair freewheeling driverless down a ramp. I watched him being hurtled across the floor with his eyes shut and a smile wrapped tightly on his face, like it was the only thing left to hold on to, saying *go on, go on* when Pietje and I tried to interrupt. I remember this scene because for a moment I looked at death and didn't turn away. I could feel it in the sockets of my eyes. Someone once compared death to the sun, because if you try to look directly at the sun it will burn out your eyes. It happens regularly to the junkies in Vondeln Park. They stare into the sun and it burns out their eyes. One has to approach this death thing obliquely, with just the sidelights on, showing Morton in a wheelchair, careering around an empty hall in a museum with his eyes shut but saying *go on go on*, because the guys are bored in the museum and want some fun and not fat women in the nude looking down from those enormous paintings on the walls. This is an image of Morton in transit, here's Mort just passing through, and it still hurts when I remember it because the background is so utterly random, Morton so utterly out of place, and it wasn't until we stopped in front of the picture Morton had brought us to Den Haag to see that I understood it was *here* my brother belonged.

It was a picture by Rembrandt, *The Anatomy Lesson of Dr Tulp*. Morton must have spent a lot of time studying this picture. He knew all kinds of stuff like the names of the guys who were in it and two of them Rembrandt hadn't meant to be there but another painter had been bribed to sneak them in later. Even the corpse had a name. Morton said he was a horsethief by the name of Aris Kindt who had been executed in Amsterdam on January 31st 1632, and the reason Aris had managed to get himself into the painting was because in those days the authorities allowed only criminals to be dissected. Rembrandt must have gone along to make drawings of the horsethief *fresh off the noose*, in Morton's phrase, the moment they cut him down, and this was how Aris Kindt alias Adriaen Adriaenson got into the picture as the corpse. In those days anatomies had to be in winter because otherwise the cadavers would stink. Morton said the winter was the season for anatomies in the same way there used to be ball and hunting seasons, with the public buying tickets to anatomies carried out in theatres just like any other entertainment, and making quite a *gezellig* occasion of the thing.

I guess my brother found some kind of comfort in the fact that we still knew the name of the guy on the autopsy table and the exact date of his death three and a half centuries after the event. It was pretty clear he identified with the corpse rather than the onlookers. I mean, there's a corpse in the picture and there are all these onlookers, and outside the picture we were also onlookers in a sense that Morton no longer was. Morton wasn't one of the onlookers. In a sense the picture was already *about* him. Outside the picture of the anatomy lesson there's this other group of onlookers around a guy in a wheelchair who wants to get into the picture as a corpse, and I remember I caught myself thinking at the time: here's Mort pulling another stunt. Tulp and the other dudes look swell in those cake-wrapper collars (Tulp with his hat on while he gives the anatomy lesson – a terrific effect of sidelight technique), but Aris lying dead on the table still steals the show. Rembrandt took a squint at the sun and came away with an image that's incredibly deathy. The star of the anatomy lesson is the corpse. You can't take your eyes off the corpse. The spring has wound down and the tune coming out of the box has stopped. There has to be a trick to it. Somehow you can't quite believe the corpse. *What's it doing?* You look for how it's different from the onlookers. So then you take a look at the onlookers and this gives you a jolt, because someone has painted you in afterwards and you realise you're looking at yourself. It's the voyeur's ultimate dream of furtive pleasure, looking with impunity through the keyhole at death. This is how it is with dead things, Morton said, this is how the instincts of living onlookers are. This is the sacrifice you demand. *You want to take the corpse apart and look inside.*

TWENTY-THREE

Take Harko. Harko's one of the onlookers. Each onlooker has a different point of view. Harko has one and I have to live with it.

Harko's version of Morton is a version of someone I never met. Harko claims to have known a guy who felt he'd been not so much born in the family in which he found himself growing up as just sort of accidentally dumped, that he grew up without acquiring a sense of a personal history, and that he never really knew who he was because he never felt he belonged. Harko says Morton once confessed this to him in as many words. I don't believe Harko. I know Morton could never have said anything like that, and it shocks me to hear someone say he did.

When Harko talks about Morton this way I feel I'm eavesdropping on Harko talking about himself. It doesn't occur to me to wonder why Morton was so fascinated by Harko's doppelgänger life.

But then there are these other moments when I recall the way Moo used to *come across* Morton standing in a room as if discovering him for the first time in her life. These memories start to get under my skin not long after my brother dies.

I have problems loving my brother, because of that twisted admiration I sometimes feel as envy, but I love him all the same and I know that he loves me. *Morton is intensely caring about me.* I'm his kid brother. I mean, what's my name? He calls me Kiddo all my life. Right? It's like Kiddo is my only name. Everyone calls me that. There aren't any problems loving me.

Launched on this undertow of a brother who cared intensely about me, Harko's version of Morton's illness is kind of subversive. I mean, I've always thought that if one of us suffered by comparison with the other, then that role of suffering-by-comparison was absolutely mine. Until Harko brought this up, it had never occurred to me, not for a single moment, that Morton was in any danger of suffering by comparison with me.

Harko asks why it was Morton who *cared intensely* about me who became ill and not me whom he cared intensely about. Why hadn't *I* got ill?

I think this is kind of a lunatic question, but when I listen to myself making an effort to answer it I feel uncomfortable and pretty foolish. I say look, *bud*dy, people don't have like a *rea*son for getting ill. They just *get* ill. Harko puts on this cool, superior tone of voice and says he's not suggesting anyone's to blame, but he's not talking about people, he's talking about Morton, and do I really believe that Morton just got ill?

This drives me crazy. I start shouting that whatever reason Morton may have had for getting ill it had absolutely nothing to do with me, and I get really angry. Whenever Harko and I talk about Morton, it often ends in a fight.

The trouble is, and there's no way round it, that there *is* some truth in this. There is some truth in Harko's argument, particularly when one's talking about a person like Morton with the kind of porous cell walls that let in everything. Morton *did* just absorb stuff, all kinds

143

of stuff, including a lot he may not have wanted to.

It's conceivable, I mean it's absolutely possible that the role of suffering-by-comparison is actually tougher when you know you're the comparison which is the cause of that suffering in another person than when you're that person yourself. If I squeeze into Morton's frame of mind, as Harko describes it, and see that just by being I'm the cause of my kid brother's feeling of inadequacy, I can imagine the hopelessness Morton might have felt.

I imagine him in the water with his hands and legs tied, drowning. It's not nice at all.

I've tried to get this thing on paper. There's one version, only partly Harko's, of *what happened to Morton* that goes like this:

1) Because their parents don't really figure in the picture, the kid brother and his big brother form a closer attachment to each other than to anyone else in the world.

2) As long as they're growing up, the roles of hero and hero-worshipper are not a problem because this is what big brothers and kid brothers are for, until

3) It turns out that the kid brother is sort of a dud and the big brother is a rising star. Relative to the speed of the rising star the dud doesn't appear to be moving, in the shadow of its brightness doesn't even make a showing at all, and the hero/hero-worshipper relationship gets to be a problem.

4) The big brother can fulfil his destiny as a rising star only at the cost of losing sight of the kid brother altogether, ending up some place worlds apart from the only person who has ever mattered to him.

I use these corny metaphors as a kind of a rehearsal to soften a point of view Harko expresses much more bluntly, like I'm not yet committing myself to this as the final thing, because it would lead me to accept Harko's conclusion that Morton invented a terminal illness for himself as the only way out of the deadlock of suffering-by-comparison, and for me this is unacceptable.

In Rembrandt's picture of *The Anatomy Lesson* you see all these onlookers gathered round a corpse, each of them with his own point of view. The group portrait of the living onlookers buzzes with all these contradictory sensations about the corpse they're looking at – reluctance, curiosity, amazement and dread, a restless swarm of flies hovering over the cadaver. Only the corpse is at rest. Only the corpse has this absolute certainty. Only the corpse can be the centre of gravity. It's like Morton was still upstaging me, even in death.

TWENTY-FOUR

One of the things from the anatomy lesson that somehow sticks in my mind is that thing about a body having
two ages. A body has not just its outside age but an
inside age, which is something only pathologists get to
see, and as the pathologist Dr Bloem saw it, Morton
looked pretty old inside. Bloem said there was a hell of
a difference between the two ages of Morton's body.
Mort was all eaten up with cancer inside. He looked old
because he was rotting with cancer, and a terrible stench
came out of the cadaver, but you could never have told
that looking at him from outside.

I'm reminded of all this when I'm reading Morton's
letter again a few years after his death. I come to the
place where he writes, 'I want you to look inside me
and rid yourself of any illusions. The illusion you must
get rid of is that any feeling can be pure, *any* feeling,' and
I can see the corpse on the table in front of me, and the
image pulls me up sharp.

I've never shown Morton's letter to anyone, not even
Pietje. Pietje and I have got together again, but on the
understanding that we don't talk about what's happened
in the past. Pietje and I don't actually live together. I
mean, things have never been quite the same between us

since Morton died, although we're still good friends.

At the end of the letter there's a passage Morton quotes from a book he'd bought in San Francisco, underlining some of the words, and I start wondering what's happened to that book.

I hunt around and find it in a drawer in Morton's desk in the attic of the house off Singel. The book is about the public anatomies that were being done in Holland in the sixteenth and seventeenth centuries, and it's illustrated with paintings that were made on this subject. Mostly it's about just one painting, Rembrandt's *Anatomy Lesson of Dr Tulp*, and this is where Mort has done most of the underlining.

The anatomy as acted by Dr Tulp and pictorially rendered by Rembrandt was part of a dramatic play that in all its particulars was carefully rehearsed with a view to its public staging. The people appearing on the canvas actually occupy the light-flooded stage at the centre of the anatomical theatre that we must imagine was surrounding them. Such theatres were designed to accommodate several hundred persons for all kinds of entertainment, among which the public anatomies were the most popular . . .

A recurrent theme in the pictorial representations of these anatomies is the idea that the dissection of the cadaver of the criminal is also a punishment for crimes . . .

The persons immediately concerned with the creation of Rembrandt's painting, Dr Tulp and the guild members, were undoubtedly conscious of the element of atonement in the public anatomy and of its ultimate metaphysical aim, the Know Thyself . . .

147

It's incredible all the stuff they know about just one picture. Beginning with the physician, Dr Nicolaas Pieterszoon Tulpius, all the guild members in Rembrandt's painting were people who actually lived at the time and can be identified by their names. What seems to have attracted Morton's interest in particular is that two of the figures don't belong to the group in Rembrandt's original painting. These two figures were added later by someone else.

The two guys who sneaked into the painting afterwards have been identified as Jacob Blok and a certain Frans van Loenen. With Frans, it's the hand that's the giveaway. It looks like one of those trick plastic hands I used to have as a kid that you hold in your sleeve, and which comes off when somebody tries to shake it. I don't know who painted Frans, but it wasn't Rembrandt. Frans is a fake.

Frans is the guy standing out at the top of the painting you see reproduced in the book. You notice him because he's on top of the pile, the only guy not facing Tulp and the corpse. Frans is looking back at you looking at him. There's an arrow pointing at this guy, which must almost certainly have been drawn by Morton, because it's marked in the same green ink which Morton used in all of his engineering designs.

I take a magnifying glass and have a closer look at this guy. I hold up a thumb and a finger to cover up the cake-wrapper collar and the beard and I suddenly see Morton's face looking back at me.

I don't know why I never noticed it before. I mean, I must have stood for quite a long time in front of the picture at the museum in Den Haag, but I never noticed the similarity. It's only after my brother dies, and I really begin to think about our relationship, that Morton's extraordinary resemblance to old Frans suddenly hits me.

Morton was absolutely right about people wanting to open up a dead body and look inside. I had nightmares about it for a long time after, and I still feel a sort of guilt. It shows up in questions like 'How come you think I killed my brother Morton?' when Harko throws stuff at me about Morton never having gone places the way everyone was expecting he would, and in a way this was my fault for having *held my brother back*. This thing has obsessed me. It's not surprising I had eyes only for the corpse, and overlooked some guy who's in the background of the picture.

The corpse still dominates *The Anatomy Lesson*. Old Aris still upstages everyone else. But after reading Morton's letter again and finding that book marked in his green ink, it's no longer Aris I'm looking at. It's this Frans van Loenen guy.

Pietje's staying out in Steenhoven while her parents are away on holiday. I call her up and tell her about the book, mentioning the two fakes in the picture, and the amazing resemblance I've noticed between Morton and this Frans van Loenen guy. I can hear Pietje sucking in her breath at the other end of the line. She tells me to come out to Steenhoven right away. There's something she wants to tell me about Frans.

TWENTY-FIVE

Pietje says, 'Morton told you about a man who came to the bar where I work, and paid me money to sleep with him. It's true. I took the money. I was hired, like a prostitute.'

She lets the sand in the cup of her hand trickle slowly through the cracks between her fingers, until it's all gone.

'The man was Morton.'

'OK. So when did this happen?'

'You don't believe me.'

'I'm just listening to you. I'm not believing. I'm not disbelieving. All I'm doing is listening to you.'

Pietje doodles in the sand with a piece of driftwood, and I watch a dark bank of cloud come sliding across the sky, casting a shadow over Steenhoven beach.

'It happened the summer the three of us met, a few weeks before Morton went to America.'

'Where was I?'

'You were working at the bar as usual.'

'OK. So I'm working at Siberia, Morton shows up at the bar where you work, pays you money to sleep with him, and afterwards we all meet and go back to your place where Morton gets more of the same thing for free. Are you telling me that's what happened?'

151

'Exactly.'

'How d'you expect me to believe that? It's ridiculous.'

'Not if there are two Mortons. Imagine there's a Morton called Frans. Imagine there's a Morton you don't know about.'

I feel sickness in my stomach.

'What don't I know about Morton?'

'There's a whole side of him you don't know about.'

'Oh, fuck *this*.'

Suddenly it's begun to rain. There are just a couple of warning drops, and then it's like a tap was turned on. Pietje and I grab our things and dash through the streets in the crashing and a downpour of hail that closes in a curtain in front of us as the storm breaks overhead. We get to the house and stand panting in the porch, watching pea-size hail rebounding from the concrete, shredding her father's beloved garden. Within a couple of minutes it's been utterly destroyed. Pietje looks on helplessly.

'When Cees gets home and sees this, it's going to break his heart.'

'That's more than you've ever succeeded in doing to your dad. I don't understand why he bothered to have children.'

'You've no idea how cruel the things are you sometimes say.'

'My dad's the same as yours.'

'No, he's not.'

Pietje unlocks the front door and we go into the house.

She drops the stuff on the living-room floor and just stands there, like she doesn't know what to do or where to go next. She looks around the room at the designer-label furniture that's now twenty years out of date, the shelves full of books her father stopped buying after he learned he had multiple sclerosis, as if any further claims on life were frozen the moment his illness moved into the house. From the forlornness of Pietje's figure turning and looking at this doom, and not knowing how to escape it, I can guess what must be passing through her mind. I have to care for Pietje, I want to hold her, I stand behind her and say, 'Let's go upstairs,' because she's now sort of my last person, Pietje's really all there's left.

Pietje's room in her parents' house is still a kiddy room, with the dolls still arranged in a cupboard, the decrepit, battered teddy bears lolling on her bed under a wall-size family photograph of a devastating formality. It hits you the way a feeling of chill hits you when you open a fridge door. The photo documents a happy family that never existed in real life. Pietje's mum and dad stand behind a boy and a girl, all of them in their swimsuits on the beach, looking at the camera with set smiles. When I'm lying in Pietje's bed I look at this picture and try to detect the seams between parents and children that would betray they're not in one photo but two, and it's a montage of people who in real life were never in the same picture at all. I lie with Pietje under the covers as the storm is ebbing, thinking about putting me and Pietje in a seamless picture, my arms around her, like I'm framing her, to keep us inside the same picture that I'd like to hang on her bedroom wall.

She says, 'Why don't you stay? They're not coming home for another week. Do you have to go into town?'

'I promised Harko I'd help him.'

'Help him with what?'

'He wouldn't say on the phone. Whatever it is – as soon as we're through I'll come back.'

We lie there with our arms around each other and after a while Pietje says, 'Would you believe Erasmus?'

'Erasmus knows about this?'

'Yes.'

'I thought no one was allowed to know the secrets between you and Erasmus.'

'This time it's different.'

Erasmus has been around since Pietje was thirteen. He knows everything that ever happened to Pietje, every day of her life, since she was thirteen. Erasmus is Pietje's name for the notebook she always has on her knee and in which she writes everything down. The back numbers of Erasmus occupy a whole wall of Pietje's room. He's the invisible scribe who's seen it all and taken it all down. There's not much you can do to challenge Erasmus. Erasmus is like God.

I go, 'Yeah, I'd believe Erasmus.'

TWENTY-SIX

Erasmus is pocket-size, a standard fifteen-by-ten format with hard gloss covers and reinforced edges. The notebook lies fat and black, a little menacing, glistening in the cone of light on the desk in Cees's study. I sit there looking at it for a while. I help myself to cigars and brandy and watch the drifts of smoke curling up under the lamp. I open the notebook reluctantly at the place where Pietje has left the marker. Pietje has stayed in her own room. She thinks it better I read this myself.

Meeting Erasmus face to face, the only person who's had this privilege, I realise with a bit of a shock what a private person Pietje is. I was aware of this before, but not the full extent of it. I'm so used to the sight of Erasmus on Pietje's knee that he's become as much a part of her as the clothes she wears. I'm used to Erasmus as a taboo subject. He's off limits. It never occurred to me until now how much of Pietje has been off limits with him.

Naturally I was curious at first. I wanted to know what Pietje secretly thought of me. I'd nag her to let me have a peek inside, but after a while I lost interest, and stopped noticing that Erasmus was even there. Everything that matters to Pietje she confides to Erasmus. I guess he's a lot closer to her than I am. Erasmus stands between Pietje and the rest of us, with his hard black covers and reinforced edges, almost as if he was there to protect her.

Imagine Pietje didn't write to Erasmus but talked to him. Imagine Pietje talking aloud to someone invisible on her knee. You'd think she was a nut. But with someone who always sits writing on her knee when there are other people around it's different, I mean, you wouldn't necessarily think of that person as a nut. It annoys people or intrigues them or they don't pay any attention. A lot of people think Erasmus is just an affectation. But when I pick Erasmus up and feel how solid he is with all the things Pietje has told him and nobody else, and I imagine Pietje telling all these things to an invisible gnome perched on her knee, he begins to feel pretty real to me. It comes to me as quite a shock to realise how private the world is she's been living in all the time I've known or thought I'd known Pietje.

This is the first thing I learn from the anatomy lesson that begins with the post mortem when my brother dies, and maybe it's more important than all the rest. I imagine the gnome I've got sitting on *my* knee, and all the stuff I'm telling him that Pietje never gets to hear about. I imagine a world congress of gnomes, exchanging all the stuff their people never told each other and then going home and passing the news on. I guess that it could be about the most sensational thing that ever happened in the world.

What Morton's gnome confides to Erasmus puts the size of this thing in perspective. Morton doesn't have a gnome sitting on his knee. It's more like Morton is sitting on the gnome's knee.

Here's how Pietje's gnome, Erasmus, tells it:

Morton shows up tonight, all dressed up in a suit and tie like she's never seen him before, and wants to buy her a

156

drink. It's the first time he's come here. She orders the drinks and tells him it's on the house, but he doesn't want it on the house. He wants to pay for it. He says: pretend I'm a customer, pretend my name's Frans. He's smiling and funny and in a good mood. So she plays along. It's fun.

Morton's different. He's not the least bit uptight. He's sophisticated, almost suave. She's never known him this way before. They pretend he's a customer and his name's Frans. Frans says he has a surprise for her. But she's not allowed to call him Morton. She's not allowed to remember anything about him. She's never met him before. Those are the rules of the game. Frans says that otherwise the surprise won't work.

They have a couple of drinks and Frans starts getting flirtatious. He tells her how he's secretly been admiring her ankles. She's sitting at the bar with a skirt on and her legs crossed, and to her it's not a secret at all. Frans has been looking down at her legs all the time. He lifts her leg onto his lap and takes off her shoe. He starts to stroke her ankle. If Frans is doing an act, it's a pretty good one.

She asks him what he does for a living, and he says he's a businessman. He's over here from America on business now. She asks if he's married and he says he has a girlfriend, and she asks how the girlfriend would react if she found out he was sitting in a hostess bar in Amsterdam stroking a girl's legs. He says it would depend on how far stroking a girl's legs went. She says, well, how far would it go? He smiles and says: what's your name? She tells him her name's Tessa. His hand goes under her skirt and he says mockingly, well, how far would it go with you, Tessa? Do girls working in hostess bars have a rule about how far they go with their customers?

Frans is pushing his hand up her thigh as he asks these questions, and she's getting a little excited. She

157

says that if she liked a customer enough she might do him a favour, but that never happened to her yet. If she liked a customer enough she might do him a special favour for free.

Frans reaches into his pocket and puts a thousand guilders on the counter and says: would you do it for that?

She says money wouldn't have any part in it, and Frans is smiling all the time as he says come on, of course it would. He has his hand in her crotch and is pushing her with his fingers while she's looking at the thousand guilders on the counter, feeling really confused. She doesn't know if she's Pietje or Tessa. Frans is saying that most things in life are never so clear-cut, but that if money's around it will always decide the issue. He says he doesn't want any favours from a girl in a hostess bar, he wants to buy the girl in the hostess bar for an hour or two, that's why he's come, to buy the girl and have sex for money. Wouldn't Tessa take the money if a customer she liked really wanted her to? She's looking at the thousand guilders on the counter and the money is exciting, she realises she wants it, and Frans knows she does. Go on, he says, take it. And she does.

They get into a cab and Frans gives the cab driver the address of a hotel on the other side of the red light district. She's beginning to have doubts about just what's going on, but Frans is talking non-stop about his business in America, doing things to her body all the time in the back of the cab, and she has his thousand guilders in her purse, and the effect of all this is hypnotic. In the cab she's the Tessa whom Frans has paid money to have sex with, and the idea she's the girl from the hostess bar the customer has bought scares her and excites her at the same time. She's got into this game a little bit at a time, but it's now gone so far she no longer knows how she got into it in the first place.

It's only when they get into the hotel room and this *Frans* stops talking and no longer has his hands on her that she decides the game has gone far enough. She still thinks it's a game. She's sure Kiddo's going to be hiding in there somewhere.

She goes into the bathroom, she opens the cupboard, she even gets down on her knees and takes a look under the bed. She's beginning to feel foolish and angry, because the game isn't funny any more. It's a cruel game. She says OK, Morton, where's Kiddo? What are you two guys up to? Where's my surprise? Morton is locking the door, and she's waiting for him to turn round and tell her what's happening. But when Morton turns round he's not smiling any more. He's taking off his belt. He looks at her and says in a funny voice, 'Morton? Kiddo? Who the hell are they, Tessa?'

TWENTY-SEVEN

Who the hell are they, Tessa?

It's four o'clock in the morning. I pour myself a glass of brandy, get up and go to the window. I look out and try to figure out the shape of the dunes as you see them from the front of the house, but it's so dark I can't make out anything at all.

D'you think Pietje's going to be OK?

I go down the corridor into Pietje's room. It's dark in there, too. I switch on the light and see Pietje asleep. Pietje's going to be fine. This story's now over and Pietje's OK, she must be, she's asleep in her own bed.

The notebook is lying spread out on the desk under the lamp. I sit down and lean into it with a sense of dread. I see the page, and the hotel room, inside a narrowing focus of a cone of light.

TWENTY-EIGHT

Morton comes over and just rips off her dress. She's so dumbfounded she doesn't do anything. He pushes her onto the bed. She fights back. Morton grabs her arm and twists it behind her back. She's helpless. She says, Morton for Christ's sake *stop* this, you're hurting me, but he forces her face down onto the bed with her arm behind her back and sits on top of her. She can't see what he's doing because she's lying face down. She hears something ripping, and then she feels something smooth, which is the tie he's ripped off, and he's tying her hands behind her back, and she's lying trussed up with Morton on top of her. She says, Morton, don't do this to me. Don't do this to me, please. He's got something in his mouth, she can hear him grunting and panting as he tries to pull the sheet out of the bed, and it must be a piece of the sheet he's got in his mouth.

She tries to show him she's calm, but she's really scared. She says don't, Morton, *please*. Listen, Morton. Listen to something I never told anyone before. Are you listening? I was raped by my own father when I was thirteen. *Listen*, for Christ's sake! Jesus, my own father raped me, don't do this, I can't, I can't, stop it, Morton, *stop it!* He grabs her hair and jerks back her head and stuffs a handkerchief into her mouth. She keeps on screaming until her throat feels like it's bleeding and the handkerchief in her mouth is soaked with blood. She hears these ripping sounds, and she's just terrified. Morton is ripping the sheet with his teeth and tearing it into strips, and then he starts tying her ankles to the end of the bed with the strips of sheet, and when he gets off she tries to roll over, which makes him really mad. Morton's gone totally crazy. He tears off the rest of her clothes and ties her arms to the legs of the bed. He must be on the other side, but she can't turn her head to see what he's doing until suddenly she feels something slashing her buttocks, a pain shoots down her legs and she thinks, *Jesus, he's whipping me.*

Morton whips her with his belt, and she can hear how it's getting him worked up, from the whimpers and sort of gargled, frothy sounds he's making. She's lying there sobbing and lacerated, and then suddenly he stops whipping her and she feels his full weight on top of her and his prick going into her anus. He calls her a whore and a slut, and starts squeezing her neck, shuddering and moaning on top of her until he comes. She's so terrified Morton's going to do even worse things to her that she lies completely still and doesn't make a sound. He keeps on saying these abusive things and writhes around on top of her and then he gets off her, and there's silence.

She can't bear the silence. She's scared out of her wits he's going to kill her. She can feel him looking at her but doesn't know where he is. She wants to look but she doesn't dare to move. The silence lasts a long time. Then she feels his hand on her ankle, and she jumps. But he doesn't do anything to her. He's just quiet and stroking her ankles.

When he's finished stroking her ankles he unties her and takes the handkerchief out of her mouth. You creep, is the first thing she says, and remembers this is what she

162

had said to her father when he'd finished raping her that night her mother was away at her aunt's funeral.

She lies curled up on her side with a pillow in her arms and cries for hours. When she's cried herself out and is no longer scared, the anger inside her starts welling up. She sees him sitting on the floor with the same hang-dog expression of self-pity on his face that her father had after he'd raped her when she was thirteen. You creep, she says, and keeps on saying it, and the word is so feeble, all words are so feeble and so thin and so *nothing* compared with the contempt she feels that she flies into a rage and attacks him. He covers his face and cowers on the ground as she kicks him and punches him, and he does nothing to try to defend himself.

She kicks him and punches him because he's put that awful feeling of *dirt* back into her. She feels the enormity of her helplessness again, the feeling of being *dirty* that already she knows is going to force her to be silent again, feeling dirty and hating herself because she's a woman and the dirt will stick with her all her life. She's crying and hitting him until she's exhausted and there's nothing left but this dirt, which she can still feel at the bottom of the emptiness inside herself.

Morton hasn't said a thing until now. Now he says: Do whatever you like with me, I'm finished, but don't tell Kiddo. Please. If you tell Kiddo it'll destroy him.

This just infuriates her, these shitty men like Morton and her dad masking their own cowardice in these appeals to spare *other people's feelings*. How about me, she asks him, what about *my* feelings? How about not destroying *me*?

Silence. There's always silence when she asks this question. No one has ever answered this question.

She loathes this man. She can't stand being in the room with this man for a minute longer. Get out, she says. Get out of this room. Get out of this country. Get out of the world. Go into a hole and die. Go anywhere. I don't care. Just *get out!*

When he's gone she just lies on the bed. Then she wants to drink a lot of alcohol. There's a mini-bar in the room with stupid little bottles of spirits. She pours them all into her, one after another, feeling worse and worse. She goes under the shower. She tries to wash the dirt off her, but the dirt won't wash away. She weeps with fury. She wants to slash her wrists and wash away all the dirt that's mixed up in her veins, but she's too drunk, and she falls asleep in the shower, and wakes up under a cold drizzle, shivering, hours later. Outside it's beginning to get light.

She gets dressed, what dress there is to put on. She has to hold up the front when she sneaks into the street and takes a cab home. She can't stand the sight of her own room. Everything there reminds her of *him*. She looks at her face and thinks it will be all right. There's nothing they will see in her face. She changes and takes the tram to Amsterdam Central. Then she gets on a train and goes out to Steenhoven, to her parents' place.

Cees is going through a bad phase. For once she's glad of all the attention her father's getting. She can hide behind the concern for Cees. Her parents hardly notice her. They're too preoccupied with another *bad phase* in her father's illness. She wears her lie. She's used to wearing it. In her room at night she looks over her shoulder at the wounds healing in the mirror, as if they belonged to someone else who was standing there.

After a couple of days Kiddo's on the phone. He's used to her taking off. He doesn't ask any questions either. *How're you doing, Pietje,* is all he asks. And she says *fine, I'm doing fine,* praying he's not going to talk to her about Morton. But Kiddo has nothing else to talk about. As Kiddo talks to her about Morton she suddenly sees what she and Kiddo have in common, and for the first time since she came out of the hotel she's able to feel sympathy for another human being. Kiddo's been tied down and abused by his brother all his life, and doesn't even know this is happening. He's never met Frans. Maybe that's going to make it even worse for him.

Kiddo tells her Morton is leaving for America. He wants to arrange a surprise send-off for his brother. He's asking her if she'd like to *contribute something to the expenses,* and she knows the moment she's been waiting for to interrupt Kiddo and tell him what happened has already passed, and so she says sure, I'll contribute my share, of course I will, and she hangs up . . .

TWENTY-NINE

It's like I'm racing back through the cone of lamplight on Cees's desk into the tunnel of my life, having to make changes all the way at split-second speed to re-circuit the entire track. Everything that was there has been wiped out. I'm hitting familiar landmarks and not recognising them, and shooting off in unexpected directions. I flash past the terrified dove Morton forced out of the cage to say goodbye to her the night he left, plunging into the darkness of Pietje's room because Pietje wanted it that way in the weeks before, and I hear Morton whispering, 'Do you think Pietje's going to be OK?' beside my bed. I see him marking exploding diagrams with a green arrow, switching the points all the way back to that house where we spent Christmas on Cape Cod and the earliest memories of the brother who intensely cared about me. I'm back there standing on the landing with Moo, but I no longer recognise the place. My earliest memories take me back to a starting point in someone else's life, not mine. I stop with a terrific jolt at this place where the tunnel ends. I'm standing there beside my mother and looking down at Morton at the bottom of the stairs. Morton's face is in close-up. I'm not even sure it's my brother's face, because it's no longer concern or sorrow or pity I see on the face. It's a look of hatred.

I walk out of the house along a beach on the other side of the ocean. There's no way I can get back to where I began. There's all that sea between. I take the body apart and look inside, and there's no way I can put it back together or bring it to life again. Parts come up out of the ocean and are scattered along the shore and there's no way they'll ever be fitted together again.

The house is silent. Somebody's been murdered in this house. I sit in the kitchen, drinking coffee as the sun goes up. I write a note to Pietje. I tear it up.

It feels like all the bones had been sucked out of my body. I have to move, or I'll fall apart. I pick up the pencil again and try to write my name.

When I go out of the house I leave the pencil and a blank piece of paper on the kitchen table.

I catch the train back to Amsterdam.

THIRTY

I've been up all night and when I get home I crash, I'm totally beat. All I want to do is sleep and get out of this for a while. I dive in and land in a puddle, all tiredness and no sleep. I flail around. I feel just yucky. I don't know what to do with my head. I don't know where to think. I tie myself into knots. I hang onto my dick and try to climb up it. I feel like I reached the end of the world and didn't stop. Only coke can handle this.

I lay myself out a real brain-beater of a line, a world-fucking snort a yard long. Queen Victoria, our old mascot in the Singel house attic now supervising things here, is looking on from the mantelpiece. I can just hear her saying something like *it's all the way downhill from here* as I hoist the snort and I think, well, throwing in a couple of XTCs as an afterthought, thank God for that.

After a while the gnome comes out. I can identify him. He's there, scribbling away on my knee. My gnome is talking to Pietje's gnome, Erasmus. I listen to Erasmus holding forth for a while, and then it's my gnome's turn. 'Dear Erasmus,' my gnome begins, 'I've been thinking about the laundry idea Pietje's been going on about all this time . . .'

I follow the words across and down the page and over the horizon with a calm, restful feeling, like there's absolute clarity. I don't remember I ever had a feeling like this before.

THIRTY-ONE

I call Harko, and he tells me to meet him in a coffee
shop off Rembrandt Plein. I've never been to the place
before. Harko shows up wearing a ridiculous hat and
dark glasses and carrying a briefcase. When he sits down
and takes this stuff off I'm horrified how he looks. He
looks as if he's been in a fight. His face is puffy. There's
rouge on his face, blue eye-shadow and lipstick. His eyes
are slits. The slits narrow a little more when he grins at
me across the table.

'Jesus, what happened to you?'

'Just take it easy.'

'Why the get-up? What *is* this?'

'Have a look and shut up, will you.'

Harko takes a piece of paper out of his pocket and
unfolds it. It seems to be the plan of a building. Harko
explains.

'Main entrance here. Side entrance here, at the opposite end of the compound. That's where we go in, getting
into the main building here, across the terrace overlooking the harbour, into the canteen. Long walk up to the
tenth floor. Can't use the elevator. Have to go by the
stairs. Corridor. Office with adjoining room here. And
that's where they are.'

'What are?'

'The platinum discs.'

'What platinum discs?'

'The platinum discs in the Shell building that I keep on telling you about. Don't you remember anything?'

'OK. I remember. The platinum discs. What about them?'

'They're in a bullet-proof glass case with a combination lock. I've been trying to get the combination for six months. Well, we have that now, don't we. And we have all the keys we need to get us up there. I'd say that makes the platinum discs available, wouldn't you? Highly available. We're in and out in twenty minutes. We walk out of the Shell building with the swag. It's dead easy.'

I go, 'Who's this we?'

'You and me.'

'Wait a minute.'

'You owe me a few favours, Kiddo.'

'I know I do. But this isn't a favour. It's lunatic. It's suicide. It won't work. We'll be sent to jail.'

'Of course it'll work.'

'Give me a week to think about it.'

'I don't have a week. I'm going in tonight.'

'No way. '

I look at Harko's puffy face. The guy's a wreck. He's thirty. He's wearing make-up, for Christ's sake. I mean, he must be really desperate. I feel sorry for Harko.

I go, 'Why does it have to be tonight? Why don't we leave it for a week, and then talk about it again?'

'Tonight's my last chance. I may not be around in a week. I may not get that far, Kiddo.'

He tosses the vodka down with some pills.

'It has to be tonight. Look . . . you don't have to come into the building with me. They have a couple of guys patrolling at night. From the harbour side you see the lights go on, and that shows where the guys are. That's all I'm asking you to do. They're moving around all the time, and I have to know where they are. You just have to watch what floor they're on, and let me know where they're going.'

'How do I do that?'

'By radio. We're in radio contact. That's all you need do, OK? Just stick around on the harbour side and keep an eye on the building, and tell me what floor the guys are patrolling for as long as I'm inside.'

'What about the dogs? I'm scared stiff of dogs.'

'What dogs?'

'What if they do patrols *out*side the building, and they suddenly show up with a bunch of dogs?'

'There *aren't* any patrols outside the building. There *aren't* any dogs.'

'OK. But what if the radio contact breaks down? I don't even know how those things work, for Christ's sake.'

'Oh, that's easy. I'll show you right now.'

My heart sinks as Harko opens his briefcase and takes out the radios. He's serious about this. He's crazy. He hands me one of the radios. It's got NATO stamped on it.

'Where'd you get these?'

'Nicked 'em from my dad. They use them on the air-bases. These things work. NATO depends on them working to get their airplanes off the ground. Satisfied?'

Harko shows me how to handle the radio and tells me to go into the lavatory and bleep him to prove to myself that it works. There's not much I can do about this. So I take the NATO radio into the john and lock myself in, and sit on the toilet and bleep him.

'Harko? It's me. Can you hear me?'

'Roger.'

'What?'

'You have to say Roger when you start and Over when you're through, to avoid confusion. Over.'

'Roger. I heard you really clearly. Look . . . don't do this, Harko. It's a big mistake. You'll regret it. Over.'

'Roger. Meet me at the Petroleum Harbour at eleven o'clock tonight. There's a company there called TTS. You'll see the name on a board at the entrance. I'll be waiting for you there. If you're not there, I'll have to go without you, Kiddo. I'm going in tonight. And one other thing. I just had to leave without paying, because I don't have any money on me right now. You're making a good investment. I'll pay you back with a platinum disc that's worth a few million dollars. Thanks. Over and out.'

'Wait a minute! Harko, you shithead—'

I sprint out into the street, but of course I'm too late. There's no sign of Harko, but I keep on running anyway, because I don't have any money on me either.

THIRTY-TWO

From downtown Amsterdam it's a hell of a long way out to the Petroleum Harbour. On my bike it takes me over an hour, and it pours with rain the whole time. I find this board with TTS written on it, and I hang out in the bushes on the side, because cars keep on passing up and down the road on the waterfront, picking out this guy loitering with his bike on a rainy night who's looking casual as hell in their headlights.

Harko shows up half an hour late in his SHELL truck. I shove the bike into the back of the truck and hop up into the cab, soaked to the skin and shivering with cold.

I go, 'Guess we'd better call it off. We'll screw up. We can't operate in this weather. Let's go home.'

'Why can't we operate in this weather?'

'Fuck, it's *rain*ing. I'm *wet*, for Christ's sake.'

'There are dry clothes in the back. My suit, if you like. Help yourself.'

I take a look at Harko. He's just staring ahead, kind of glazed. He can hardly hold the wheel. Harko's loaded to the eyeballs.

I go, 'It's no good, Harko. They'll arrest you the moment you get out of the truck. You're not even going to get there. You can't even drive.'

'You drive, then.'

'I don't know how to drive.'

'What?'

174

'I haven't learned to drive. I don't have a licence.'

'I'll teach you.'

'No.'

Harko stares ahead and says in a dead-pan voice, 'You're going to be driving this truck in five minutes. If you don't, I'll kill you, Kiddo.'

I listen to the wipers going back and forth. I listen to Harko. Harko has an unpredictable streak. He can have a pretty mean side. I try to find the right tone of voice for this.

I go, 'Don't talk crap, Harko,' in a cheerful, don't-be-such-a-nit sort of voice. 'It wouldn't be worth it. It really wouldn't. I mean, I'm perfectly happy to learn to drive. I don't *mind*. I don't mind at all. If you want me to give it a try, sure, we'll give it a try.'

The rain crashes on the roof of the truck. Harko doesn't say anything for a couple of minutes.

'There's a tin in the compartment.'

I reach into the compartment and hand him the tin. Harko takes out some pills and swallows them.

'Platinum discs. You should see 'em. A whole fucking case, full of platinum discs.'

I perk up. I get really bright and enthusiastic. I go, 'I *bet*. I mean, I can imagine. It must be a hell of a sight.'

'Maybe the driving lesson isn't a good idea,' goes Harko. 'Maybe the whole thing isn't a good idea.'

He wraps his arms round the steering wheel and rests his chin on his hands. 'Coming along Prins Hendrik Kade on the way here I saw the Shell building across the harbour. Beautiful, beautiful building. And honest, you know what I thought? I thought: you're never going to beat that fucker. No way will you beat those guys. You can forget your dogs. There are cameras all over that beautiful building. There are heat-seeking devices that smell people out and set off alarms. The whole fucking building is wired. We'd go in and burn. We'd get ourselves fucking roasted. We wouldn't get anywhere near those platinum discs. We wouldn't have a chance in hell. Time for a spot of ROSCSO, as they say at Shell. Review overall situation and consider strategic options.'

'Yeah, well . . .'

'The overall situation. I'm not on top of it any more. It's not the lark it was. I no longer can tell if the bloke I'm seeing with his knickers down at office meetings is there or if I'm imagining him. I can no longer keep him and me apart. I must have made a gaffe and didn't even notice it. Maybe I went in to work and still had my make-up on. I don't remember. Just take today and the way I've been acting. Today was par for the course. At Shell I've been given my notice. I'm broke. I'm a junkie. I don't have anywhere to live. My girlfriend's dumped me. The strategic options . . . got a cigarette on you?'

Harko inhales and blows a cloud of smoke at the windshield.

'What are the strategic options, Kiddo?'

'I don't know. Are there any?'

'Only one. The Jelinek Clinic. Get on a programme.'

'Sounds like a good idea, Harko.'

'Uppers and downers, innit. It's fucking crazy. Best fucking market in the world to get screwed doing drugs, best fucking clinic with the best fucking programme to get yourself unscrewed.'

Harko winds down the window and throws the cigarette out.

'Let's go.'

He starts the truck, and somehow we drive back into Amsterdam.

It's around three in the morning when we get to the Jelinek Clinic. That's the great thing with the welfare programme in Holland. You can sign on at any time of the night or day, they always receive you with open arms. Harko abandons the truck under the No Parking sign at the entrance, and I watch the door close behind him.

176

THIRTY-THREE

In the kitchen I take the jars down from the shelf and put them on the table. I hunt around for something to carry them in. Somewhere around there should be a stay-cool styrofoam container. I bought it when I moved into this place and saw myself getting into serious housekeeping, with shopping lists and stuff like that. I bought it on the off chance that something might come of it, but nothing did, and now I need it I can't find the damn thing.

The phone rings. Pietje's voice comes flooding through. I can hear the relief in her voice.

'I've been trying to get you all night.'

'Yeah, I know. I was out with Harko.'

'I was worried something bad had happened.'

'The gnomes must have been talking to each other.'

'What?'

'I'll explain later.'

'Are you OK?'

'Terrific. I don't have to go to jail after all.'

'Is Harko in jail?'

'He just turned himself in at the Jelinek.'

'Poor Harko. What are you doing?'

'Right now I'm considering my strategic options. Remember that stay-cool styrofoam container I once bought? I can't find it.'

'It's in the oven.'

'*That's* where it is. So maybe I'll – look, when's the next train out to the coast?'

'They leave Amsterdam Central around the half hour every hour. There should be one leaving around half past five. Are you coming?'

'I have a bit of luggage. Could you pick me up in the car?'

'I'll be there.'

I hang up, listening to the echo of that *I'll be there.* Here's three reasons for loving a girl like Pietje. She knows when to call. She knows when not to call. She knows where the stay-cool styrofoam container is.

There are five jars on the kitchen table, containing around twenty percent of what used to be inside Morton, according to Dr Bloem. I pack the jars in the container and shut the lid. On the container it says the stay-cool is also airtight. I don't really know what I have in mind. I'm doing this without thinking about it too much. I pick up the container. It feels pretty heavy.

It's a cold, wet day. Outside I feel the moisture on my face. Moisture drips from the trees as I walk along the canal. I stand in a light drizzle, waiting for the tram. The first tram doesn't come until it's almost five.

Amsterdam Central is deserted at this time of the morning. I'm a sucker for deserted stations early in the morning. I love them. There's a much stronger sense of setting out on a journey when you're waiting for a train to pull in at an empty platform. You feel the early morning cool and look at the emptiness inside the open-ended iron and glass hangar of Amsterdam Central, and you can have the idea you're setting out on a journey at the beginning of the world. Pietje will be waiting at the other end when the train arrives, and I'll get into the car, and I'll say to her, already I know I'll say to her, Pietje, let's go to the sea.

THIRTY-FOUR

We stop off at the house to pick up the wetsuit and flippers, before driving on through Steenhoven along the
coast. We don't talk much. Pietje hums softly as she
drives, twisting a coil of hair round her finger.

She turns off the road and drives along a track into the
dunes. The track dips into a hollow and ends on a knoll
overlooking the sea.

A ceiling of cloud hangs low over the ocean. There's
no wind. The solid sea and sky don't seem to move, as if
they'd been turned to stone. Sea and sky stretch out to
the horizon, gray and inert, as if they were dead.

We take the stuff out of the car and go down to the
beach. Pietje has a thermos with coffee. We sit in a hollow in the dunes, smoking and drinking coffee, watching
two specks growing larger as they splash towards us
along the shore.

The specks come into shape as a man and a dog. The
man calls out something we can't understand as he's
passing. He waves and points up at the sky. We wave
back.

Immediately the dog veers out, snout to the ground,
heading straight for the wetsuit and the stay-cool styrofoam container standing down on the high-water line.

The dog sniffs around the container and suddenly raises a leg to pee on it. *Oy*, I shout, picking up a stone to throw at the dog, and with a start he bounds away.

When I get undressed I feel the cold. The old wetsuit that belongs to Cees hasn't been used in a long time. The rubber is brittle and webbed with cracks. I wash it out in the sea, kneading the rubber to soften it so as I can put the suit on more easily. Sitting on the beach, I pull on the flippers, and go back to pick up the container.

Pietje has wandered off down the shore. She's already a hundred yards off. She stops and crouches. I can't tell which way she's facing. I wave to her, but she doesn't see me. I lift the container and walk backwards, splashing into the sea.

I feel the rush of cold water around my feet. I keep on wading backwards until I'm up to my waist. Water leaks through the cracks in the wetsuit and trickles cold down my legs. I hold the styrofoam container in the sea to find out if it's going to float or sink.

It floats. I push it under, and despite its weight it comes floating up again. I push the container out in front of me, kicking out with my flippers. There's enough air inside the box to keep my arms buoyed up as I swim on, slowly, pushing it out to sea.

As I keep on swimming, my body gets warmer. I'm sinking and rising on the light heaving of the ocean that you don't see when you're looking out from the shore. Rising and falling with the swell, I feel I'm part of its exhalations and inhalations, part of a vast diaphragm of the ocean that is breathing around and under me.

Treading water, I turn and look back. The shore is already so remote it seems unreal. In the sea I am alive with a sharp sense of urgency. The sense of my own body, buoyant in the deep and cold expanse of ocean surrounding me, is much more real. I rise on the feeling

180

of my weightlessness. The ocean seems so much higher than the land. It seems as if I'm looking down from a wall of water, a standing flood towering on the edge of the land and about to topple over.

I scan the empty beach. The car is already a speck in the dunes. I try to make out a shape that may be Pietje or shadow or just driftwood. I see it indistinctly, moving and then not moving on the shore.

It's either me or him.

I open the lid of the box, and turn it over.

At once the sea reaches in, washing out the jars containing Morton's inner organs preserved in methyl alcohol. I pull the box away. For a few moments the jars bob on the surface. Then they disappear.

Somehow I don't believe that the jars can have gone down. I have an uneasy feeling they'll come bursting up out of the ocean. I swim round and round the patch of sea where the jars have disappeared. We never get shot of family ties. We think we do. It's just that we can no longer see them. We draw away from them, and the ripples just move with us, and then the circles are ahead of us, getting wider and wider.

I tread water, looking all around me in search of floating jars. I have the unpleasant illusion I'm looking at glass jars wherever I catch sight of glints of light flashing on the crests of the waves. I put the lid back on the box, using it as an air cushion, and swim round in ever wider circles, waiting for something to happen.

Ten minutes pass, half an hour. But no jars float back up. Soon I've lost track of the patch where they sank. The jars with my brother's remains have gone to the bottom of the sea.

I laugh. I cackle with glee. I'm no longer encumbered. Buoyed up on an empty airtight float, I'm moving more easily in the water. I'm alone out at sea, but I'm unafraid. I'm living here and now. The water's cold and my body feels numb, but I just want to keep on swimming.

I feel an extraordinary lightness. I don't want to go back. I want to swim for ever.

I turn away from the land, feeling the pull of the tide towards the horizon, and I swim on out to the open sea.

THIRTY-FIVE

'Dear Erasmus, I've been thinking about that laundry idea Pietje's always on about. I'd like you to use your influence on this. You've got to talk to her about it. I don't see an awful lot of future in Pietje's situation. She must stop working in bars and do something with her life, especially now that Morton has dropped out of the picture, and this other guy has stepped into his place. I feel someone has to apologise to Pietje. Someone has to say they're sorry for what Frans has done. I could say Morton wasn't able to help himself, I could say it's a pity, *because Morton was such a beautiful guy,* but saying that doesn't help us either. We have to cut Morton loose. We must get all that behind us. We must operate on the cancer and wipe it out. I think Pietje taking her washing back home is not such a hot idea. There are stains we can never get rid of, and the doom will keep on showing through. We should get away from the sea. Pietje could open that laundry she's always been talking about. I don't know that Amsterdam will be the best place for this. Sometimes I wake up at night and I hear the sea groaning behind the dykes. Morton must have heard it too, only it was inside himself, and it got too loud, and when Morton cracked up the sea came in. Pietje and I should get away from Amsterdam. We should head inland. I can imagine there's a place in the Dutch mountains where Pietje could open her laundry. I've never been down south myself, but people who have been say the mountains are quite substantial. OK, I mean, not enormous, but a lot taller than you'd expect in a country that's mostly below sea level and in constant danger of flooding. She'll miss the sea at first, because she's lived there all her life. But we ought to get away from the sea and head for that place in the Dutch mountains, I mean, we should do that quite soon . . .'